Media's
The Taxman Cometh

"I love a novel that's funny, and *The Taxman Cometh* is very funny, delightfully well-written, yet with a serious message about how government bureaucracy affects us all. Read. Enjoy. And if a comparison to Catch 22 pops into your mind, that's not surprising."
—Marvin Kalb, award-winning reporter CBS and NBC News for 30 years, founding director, Shorenstein Center for Press and Public Policy, Harvard's Kennedy School of Government, best-selling author

"There have been brilliant satires about the tax bureaucracy before, from the Beatles song 'The Taxman' to the film 'Harry's War,' but in some ways Jim Greenfield's *The Taxman Cometh* outdoes them all. His tale of a little guy who can't take it anymore is both compelling and timely, given the tax scandals we read about in Washington almost every day."
—John Fund, National Review Online columnist senior editor, *The American Spectator*

"Jim Greenfield's *The Taxman Cometh* will undoubtedly put a smile on the face of even the most dedicated big government freeloader. In the 'Everyone Deserves a Trophy' society we live in, it's refreshing to know that Jim's literary voice will cut through the politics, using the American spirit of a used car dealer."
—Lars Larson, syndicated radio host Compass Media Networks

"During 14 years in Congress I forced official hearings that exposed a startling abuse of power, lies, harassment, and brute force by the IRS against American citizens. I wrote three books on the subject, including in 1984, 'To Harass Our People,' which sold over one million copies. I was rewarded for daring to criticize the IRS with a criminal prosecution and conviction that was later overturned by the U.S. Supreme Court – but not before I served 15 months in federal prison. *The Taxman Cometh* is fictional, but this compelling story is no worse than today's scandalous IRS abuses in the real world. I can only hope the government doesn't retaliate against the author, Jim Greenfield, for telling the truth, like they retaliated against me."

— **Congressman George Hansen** – represented Idaho's 2nd district 1965 to 1969 and 1975 to 1985

"In *The Taxman Cometh*, a modern-day David stands up for liberty against bureaucratic Goliath. With the backdrop of real-life IRS scandals, you'll enjoy this compelling story so much that you'll scarcely notice you're being shown a vision of how the future could look without Goliath in our lives."

—Steve Buckstein, founder, Cascade Policy Institute

Foreword

With its huge bureaucratic state and high taxes, the framers of the Constitution wouldn't recognize today's America as the republic they founded. *The Taxman Cometh* ends with a prescient quote from Thomas Jefferson: "To preserve the people's independence, we must not let our rulers load us with perpetual debt!" I've spent the last thirty years following this admonition, fighting against wasteful government spending and high taxes.

Jefferson recognized that government officials would never voluntarily constrain spending and limit their own power, and understood that excessive public spending leads to taxation and oppression. But Jefferson and the other Founding Fathers would be shocked to see how far modern America has travelled down the road to serfdom. Today ordinary citizens are turned into criminals for trying to protect themselves from a government that seizes their money, property, and liberty. This is what happens to the hero of *The Taxman Cometh*, who courageously stands up to the ridiculously stupid bureaucracy that all Americans live under today.

Americans should be on guard against politicians who recklessly spend money, and then tell us it's our patriotic duty to pay more taxes to fund their corrupt, never-ending extravagance. Our government has a spending problem. You can't solve a spending problem by raising taxes.

Statists justify extravagant government spending and huge budget deficits with a theory they call "Keynesian" economics. According to Keynesian theory, if the government takes money from you and me by force, and gives it to the president's friends at Solyndra, this stimulates the economy. Keynesians believe that if you take a bucket of water from a lake, then walk around to the other side of the lake and dump the water back in, it will stimulate the lake. This is supposed to make us all richer. Politicians love Keynesian economics because it gives them an excuse to take our money and hand it out to people who contribute to their campaigns. Now the people who receive this money don't think it's wasteful; they think it's great. But the taxpayers from whom the money is taken don't think it's that great.

Keynesian economics is a brilliant theory. The only problem is that it doesn't work. Keynesian policies make the wealth-producing private sector smaller, and the wealth-destroying government bureaucracy bigger. And the big government politicians who demand that you pay more taxes are as insistent and monomaniacal as a teenage boy on a prom date. They lure you in by claiming they only want to tax the rich. This sounds good if you aren't rich. But middle class working folks soon find that they are the ones paying those "taxes on the rich."

The only way to get the government back within its constitutional limits is to reduce the source of its power, i.e. taxes. If we cut taxes we can shrink government to a level where it can be drowned in ..., well, if not a bathtub, at least maybe a swimming pool. We must defeat politicians who tell us that we peasants aren't sending enough cash in for the king to spend.

We often hear politicians say we need to restore trust in government; in other words, restore trust in *them*. Our founders didn't trust government. Why, in an age of massive systemic public corruption, should we? This novel is fictional, but it's realistic enough to be powerful satire. And it definitely doesn't restore trust in government.

The Taxman Cometh isn't some ponderous academic work about taxation and economic policy. It's just a great story about an ordinary citizen, Sam Samson, the guy at whom those IRS guns on the front cover are pointed, who only wants one thing from the government. Like millions of taxpayers who don't ask for handouts, he just wants to be left alone. But the government won't leave Samson alone. And when they take everything he has, including his liberty, he goes to war against the oppressors.

This thought-provoking novel portrays the absurdity of our overbearing government bureaucracy with a story that is entertaining and fast-paced. *The Taxman Cometh* will become part of our national dialogue about taxes and freedom. And it's funny as hell. Author Jim Greenfield is a cross between Ayn Rand and Monty Python. If enough people read this hilarious "man versus state" book, the IRS will be put out of business, which is okay with me.

Grover Norquist,
President, Americans for Tax Reform

The author wants all readers,
especially any who happen to be IRS agents,
to know that this story is not autobiographical.

The TAXMAN Cometh

Notes from the Underground Economy

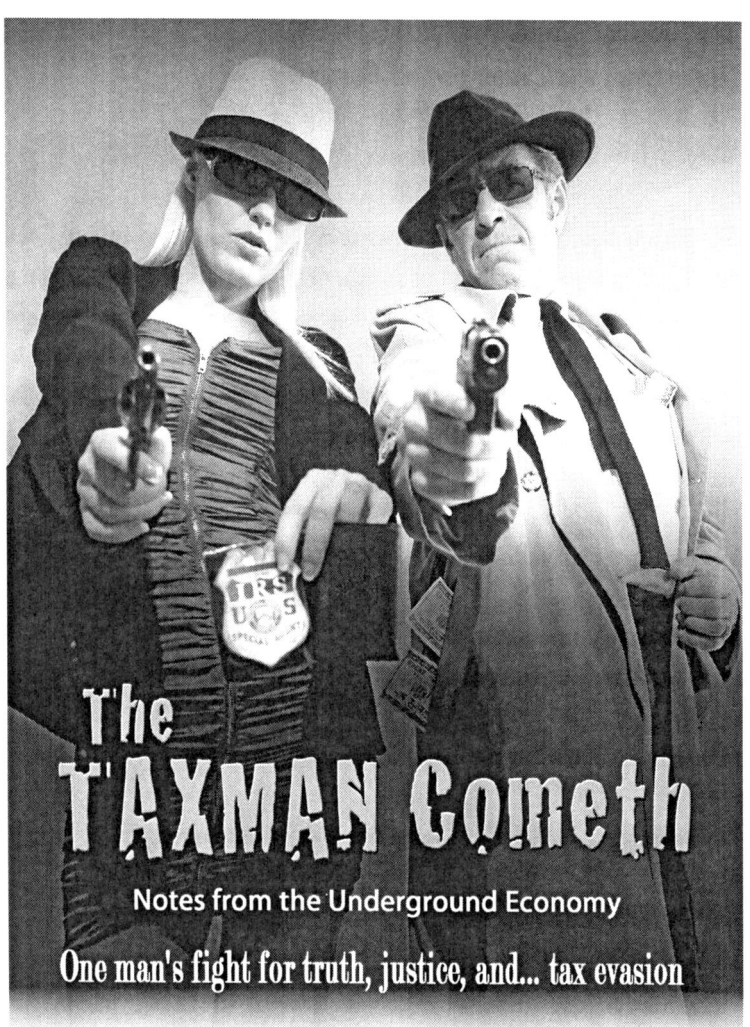

The Novel

Jim Greenfield

Line of Fire Productions
Portland, Oregon

The Taxman Cometh
Notes from the Underground Economy

©2013 Jim Greenfield

No part of this book may be reproduced or transmitted in any form or by any means, electronic or mechanical, including photocopying, recording, or by an information storage and retrieval system—except by a reviewer who may quote brief passages in a review to be printed in a magazine, newspaper, or on the Web—without permission in writing from Line of Fire Productions.

For information, please contact:
Line of Fire Productions
Portland, Oregon
info@taxmancometh.net
website: www.taxmancometh.net

Printed and bound in the United States of America.

Published by Line of Fire Productions. All rights reserved.

ISBN: 978-0-9910577-0-2
LCCN: 2013953011

Cover and author photo by Colleen Cahill, Cahill Studio
Cover and interior design by Juanita Dix

Acknowledgments

Thanks to Steve Buckstein, who's believed in this project for 23 years (no kidding), to Ben Greenfield for his insightful feedback, to Sue Collier for editing, Wes Harris and Carly Kingston for looking like real IRS special agents, to Juanita Dix for the great looking cover, Kristen Eckstein for bringing it all together, and to Grover Norquist for leading the charge.

Dedication

In the spirit of Ayn Rand, I dedicate this book to myself; may I finally get the recognition I deserve. Okay, just kidding. To my children, whose names I won't mention to protect you from whack jobs. May your generation lead our nation back to freedom – but don't expect it to be easy.

*"Let me tell you how it will be.
One for you, nineteen for me.
Should 5 percent appear too small,
be thankful I don't take it all.
'Cause I'm the Taxman, yeah,
I'm the Taxman.
And you're working for no one but me."*

—The Beatles

Tax evasion is an odd felony. It's the only crime where you go to jail, not for taking other peoples' money, but for trying to keep other people from taking *your* money.

Introduction from Author

I do something in this book authors aren't supposed to do, something I was advised by a very smart literary agent (Alice Martell) to definitely *not* do. I repeatedly interrupt this fictional story with nonfiction digressions. These digressions are labeled "Dubious Philosophical Musings Tangentially Related to the Story...." Successful writers never do this for the obvious reason that it, like, annoys the reader. I was urged by everyone who has any sense to remove these distractions from my novel. I stubbornly ignored this good advice. I consider the compelling insights in these philosophical musings to be essential to human understanding if things are ever to be set right in this confused, miserable world. So, for the sake of humanity, despite considerable personal sacrifice, I left these musings in. The price I pay may be that it keeps my novel off the bestseller list.

Anyway, the point is, if you're not interested in public policy and political philosophy, and you'd rather just read the story without interruption, you can skip over these "Dubious Philosophical Musings" as they contribute nothing to the plot. On the other hand, if you do decide to read them, please don't kvetch that it's distracting, because, like I say, it's optional. If you want to know the real reason I included these musings, the self-serving shtick about serving humanity aside, or if you don't believe me that these insights are essential to human understanding, how about this as a reason to read these passages: I spent hours writing them so, damn it, you can spend a few minutes reading them! Besides, they're included in the price of the book, so if you don't read them, you won't get your money's worth.

Preface: The Tax

"History is the record of the crimes, follies, and misfortunes of mankind."
—Edward Gibbon

"If it ain't broke, don't fix it."
—Unknown

The original U.S. Constitution, which worked pretty well for a spell, placed restrictions on "direct taxes," effectively preventing passage of an income tax. The constitutional prohibition on income taxes restrained the growth of government by making it difficult for the government to raise large amounts of money. The Founding Fathers regarded income taxes as oppressive and inquisitorial. Don't bother to look up "inquisitorial." It means "pertaining to a trial, with one person or group inquiring into the facts and acting as both prosecutor and judge," or "resembling an inquisitor in harshness or intrusiveness." Think: the Spanish Inquisition. If you've ever been audited by the IRS, you probably have a feel for what "inquisitorial" means. (You may even have a feel for what "the Spanish Inquisition" means.) The Founding Fathers opposed income taxes because they didn't want us to be oppressed by government inquisitions into our finances. The Founding Fathers were very smart.

Except for a brief period during the Civil War, there was no income tax in the United States until 1913. In 1894 Congress passed an income tax, but in 1895 the U.S. Supreme Court struck it down as unconstitutional.

In 1913 Congress cleverly got around the Court's decision by passing the 16th Amendment, which, after ratification by the states, gave Congress the power to impose taxes on income. The 16th Amendment ended the era in which Americans were free from government inquisitions into their finances.

The 16th Amendment had unintended consequences. The income tax, along with the creation of the Federal Reserve Bank at around the same time, effectively overthrew the concept of limited government embodied in our Constitution by providing the central government with a limitless source of funds. The effect over the past 100 years has been to fundamentally transform the American political economic system by re-allocating vast resources from the private sector to the government. In 1995 President Bill Clinton proclaimed that the era of big government is over. He was wrong; the era of big government is *not* over. The era of big government *began* in 1913.

When Congress was debating the 16th amendment, according to the Congressional Record, four arguments were advanced in favor of an income tax:

1. The tax will only be used in time of war.
2. The tax rate will never exceed 6 percent.
3. The tax will only be imposed on the very wealthy, i.e. those in the top 1 percent of income earners.
4. The income tax will reduce the national debt.

All four of these arguments proved to be false:
1. The tax is not just used in time of war but exists in perpetuity.
2. The tax rate is way over 6 percent.

3. The tax is not just imposed on the wealthy but on almost all wage earners.
4. The tax did not reduce the national debt.

Middle-class voters in 1913 didn't know that history would show that all the arguments for the income tax were false. They were persuaded by politicians that the tax would only hit the wealthy, not themselves. Talk about getting hoisted by your own petard. This isn't unusual; it's common for taxes to be popular with those who expect them to be paid by someone else.

The income tax has not delivered on its promise to reduce the national debt. In 1913, the national debt was $1 billion. As of this writing, the national debt is $17 trillion. In other words, since the voters were first promised that the national debt would be reduced, the national debt has increased by a multiple of 17,000, or 1,700,000 percent. Since the argument was first made in 1913, politicians have frequently repeated the promise to reduce the national debt by raising tax rates. In practice, raising tax rates has never reduced the national debt. Quite the contrary; as tax rates have gone up, so has the national debt.

In 1913 Congress also created the Federal Reserve Bank for the purpose of managing the nation's money supply. In the 43-year period prior to creation of the Fed and the income tax, from 1870 to 1913, the U.S. economy grew 11 percent per year, about five times the rate at which it grows today. The inflation rate prior to creation of the Fed was zero. The dollar did not lose any purchasing power from the time of our founding until 1913. By contrast, since the creation of the Fed, the dollar has lost 96 percent of its purchasing power. A dollar today can purchase what 4 cents purchased in 1913. A candy bar that cost

4 cents in 1913 would cost $1 today. If the mission of the Fed was to maintain the value of the dollar, it has not been spectacularly successful.

When George Washington was president, the entire federal government consisted of four small cabinet-level departments. Attorney general was a part-time job. Today the attorney general, as head of the Department of Justice, has 105,000 employees. The total number of federal employees is more than 4.4 million. The total number of government employees—federal, state, and local combined—is more than 23.8 million. By way of comparison, there are only 12 million employed in manufacturing—about half the number employed by government.

From the founding of our republic in 1789 until 1913, the federal government raised the limited amounts of money it needed through tariffs on imports. With no income tax and no central bank, the power of the federal government was constrained by lack of money. The government remained small, consuming on average about 3 percent of GDP. Since 1913 the federal government has grown exponentially. Today it consumes about 25 percent of GDP and has a budget of $3.8 trillion, and annual budget deficits of more than $1 trillion. State and local governments consume an additional 15 percent of GDP. In total, approximately 40% of gdp goes to the government.

In order to allow the IRS to collect taxes from taxpayers who might otherwise be disinclined to pay, the federal courts have allowed the IRS to exercise certain "ultra-Constitutional" powers. Only the IRS is allowed to seize property without a warrant, prior hearing, or adjudication by a court of law. Only the IRS and Treasury Department are allowed access to private banking records without a court-ordered subpoena and without notice to the citizen who is being targeted. These extraordinary powers violate the fourth and fifth amendments of the Constitution. But that's okay, because they're the IRS.

Since the income tax and the Federal Reserve Bank were created, the rate of GDP growth in the United States has declined from 11 percent per annum to under 2 percent.

In the 100-year period before the income tax and Fed were created, the United States fought two foreign wars, lasting a total of less than three years. In the 100 years since these "reforms," we have fought seven major foreign wars, lasting a total of 40 years. During 27 of the past 50 years, the United States has been fighting foreign wars, including the Vietnam War, which lasted 12 years, and the Afghanistan War, which has now gone on for 13 years, and is still going. These never-ending wars kill our soldiers, drain our treasury, turn foreign nations against us, and have accomplished little of value for our nation. Before the income tax our government didn't have the funds to wage these kinds of wars without end.

As of 2009, the IRS had 88,203 full-time employees. To enforce Obamacare's mandatory health insurance provision, the IRS is adding an additional 16,000 agents. If you choose not to buy health insurance, one of them may soon be knocking at your door.

According to Politifact.com, Americans spend a total of about $400 billion per year for tax preparation and other costs of compliance with the tax code. According to *Forbes* magazine, taxpayers spend about 6.1 billion hours per year on record keeping, tax return preparation, and other requirements of compliance.

Approximately 2,000 Americans per year are convicted of tax crimes, such as tax fraud, failure to file a tax return, or tax evasion. Prison sentences range from two to five years. These people are imprisoned, not for stealing other peoples' money, but for trying to hang onto their own. Included among those imprisoned is movie star Wesley Snipes, who served three years for failing to file a tax return, a misdemeanor. It is IRS policy to prosecute celebrities like Snipes to generate publicity and scare ordinary folks into compliance.

Apparently the IRS doesn't feel the same way about prosecuting high-level government officials. Included among the powerful politicians who have cheated on taxes and faced no prosecution are:

- Congressman Charles Wrangle, formerly the Chairman of the House Ways and Means Committee, which, ironically, oversees federal tax policy
- Former Senate Majority Leader Tom Daschle
- The former Treasury Secretary himself, Timothy Geithner

When the Senate confirmed Geithner's appointment, cheating on taxes was not deemed to be a disqualifier for heading the government agency that oversees the IRS. Perhaps the Senate felt that Geithner's experience cheating on taxes would better qualify him to make sure that the rest of us don't.

The policy of selectively not enforcing tax laws against powerful politicians violates one of our founding principles: equality before the law. Some people want to see Wrangle, Dashle, and Geithner put in jail in the name of equality. I'd rather see people like Wesley Snipes released. In the name of equality, perhaps all our fellow citizens who are being held in IRS debtor prisons should be set free.

Jim Greenfield

Chapter 1

Brave New World

"Government is an association of men who do violence to the rest of us."
—**Leo Tolstoy**

"You don't know the power of the dark side."
—**Darth Vader**

Six thousand IRS special agents sat in a huge assembly hall in the massive U.S. Treasury Building in Washington, D.C., talking among themselves while waiting to receive their orders from the IRS commissioner. There's a difference between "special" agents and ordinary agents. Ordinary agents are accountants. They go over financial records and tax returns, and conduct audits. They are unarmed. Special agents are law enforcement officers. They carry badges and guns, seize property, and arrest people. If ordinary IRS agents show up at your door, you're going to have a bad day. If special agents show up at your door, you're going to have a bad decade.

Among the special agents assembled in the auditorium was Elliott Mess, one of the most effective and ruthless tax collectors in the agency. By coincidence, Mess looked like Robert Stack who famously played Treasury Agent Elliott Ness in the

1960s TV series, "The Untouchables." Mess intentionally accentuated the "Elliott Ness" image by always dressing in a dark 1930s-style three-piece suit, trench coat, and fedora hat, as a result of which he was frequently mistaken for the real Elliott Ness. Being confused with Elliott Ness always irritated him, despite the fact that he dressed that way on purpose.

When the IRS commissioner walked onto the stage the murmuring stopped. The commissioner, a large, muscular man, darkly clad, strode to the lectern. As is common among powerful men, he spoke softly, confident that his listeners would pay attention. His voice was deep, resonant, and commanding. "My fellow enforcement officers," he began, "effective immediately, we are implementing Phase One of the Plan for Universal Compliance with the Tax Code, known in short as 'the Plan.' The Plan will fundamentally transform America. You, the Special Forces enforcement vanguard in the most powerful tax collection agency in history, will make the goal of forcing the rich to pay their fair share, not just a lofty ideal, but a cold hard reality.

"Is it fair that a few greedy people should have a monopoly on political influence, and live lives of extravagant luxury and wretched excess, while others don't have enough to eat? Wealth inequality is our nation's scourge, the social injustice at the root cause of problems like racial discord, poverty, lack of healthcare, poor quality education, crime, and drug abuse.

"The work you do is transformative. Politicians may *talk* about leveling the playing field, but you are the ones who will make it happen. The simple principle 'from each according to his ability; to each according to his needs' is the foundation of modern civilization, embodied in our progressive tax code.

Under the Plan, the age-old egalitarian dream of forcing the rich to share their wealth for the benefit of the entire society is at last coming to fruition. And to raise the additional revenue our government needs to attain social justice, the definition of 'rich' has been expanded to include not just those in the top one percent of income earners, but the top 50 percent.

"Today is the beginning of a New Order, which embodies our principles of fairness and equity. The old order is gone. The old rules are gone. The limits on our power have been swept away. The public does not yet understand the changes sweeping our nation behind the scenes. But you, the elite corps of tax collection enforcement in the world, have a central role in those changes. And the role you play puts this agency at the center of power in the new regime."

The commissioner's words produced a buzz of excitement throughout the hall. The assembled agents had heard rumors about the New Order for months, and now it was finally happening. But Elliott Mess reacted with ambivalence. The Plan, the New Order, and the commissioner's speech, reflected everything Mess believed. He thought that as a veteran special agent, with one of the most impressive enforcement records in the agency, he could play an important role in the new power structure. But Mess had been around long enough to see leaders come and go. Plans are great, but whether the commissioner could pull it off remained to be seen.

"The success of our mission rests on your shoulders," the Commissioner continued. "Are there any questions?"

An agent in the middle of the auditorium moved to a microphone in the aisle: "How do we deal with those who are uncooperative, sir?"

"We crush them," the commissioner replied, pounding his fist on the lectern in a manner out of sync with his call for social justice and the still calm intonation in his voice. Then he paused, as if recognizing that the fist pounding might have been perceived as an overreaction, and added, "There will initially be pockets of resistance. But the sooner the public understands that resistance is futile, the quicker the transition to universal compliance. Then everything will be under control."

A tall, thin, ungainly special agent with glasses, leaning over a microphone in the back of the auditorium, cleared his throat and said, "Commissioner, I think you know we all support you and your new plan. But frankly, sir, we've come under tremendous fire from Congress for improper conduct by our Exempt Organizations unit, you know, targeting political groups with out-of-date ideas, who oppose our agenda. You know what I'm talking about, sir. Some of our people have gotten into trouble for these abuses. If we enforce this new plan for, like you say, universal compliance, I mean how—how do we know we won't be the next ones on the firing line?"

"Because I've got your back," the Commissioner shot back. "I can't disclose this information now. But you will soon understand that the forces in Congress, and in the media, who led the charge against us on these so-called scandals, those forces will soon be silenced. I take full responsibility for what's going to happen, and as we go into battle, I ask you to trust me. There's no doubt we will win"

Another special agent asked, "How do we select our initial targets, sir? Should we start with the super rich?"

"No, no! Leave the super rich alone. We need them on our side—at least during the first phase. After the new order is established, we can deal with the super rich from a position of power so we can subordinate them and appropriate their wealth. But for now, the masses need to see that ordinary people like themselves have to comply with the code. Start with greedy, unscrupulous, local businessmen who deal in *cash!*"

Chapter 2
Fistful of Dollars

"The individual has always had to struggle to keep from being overwhelmed by the tribe."
—Nietzsche

"There are many things in life that are more important than money. And they all cost money."
—Fred Allen

At the very moment the IRS commissioner was speaking about greedy, unscrupulous businessmen who deal in cash, one such greedy, unscrupulous businessman who dealt in cash sat at his desk on the other side of the country, counting the 28 one hundred dollar bills that had just been handed to him by a customer. Sam Samson was oblivious to the Plan for Universal Compliance being launched by the IRS that day in Washington. Samson was in his element; smoking a cigar, feet on his desk, doing what he did best: selling used cars

In his early forties, Samson was an athletic and good looking guy, dressed in a silk sports jacket with a pocket handkerchief, blue jeans, and well-shined leather boots. He handed a set of car keys and certificate of title to the customer who had just paid him and stuffed the cash in his pocket.

Samson was the owner of Spoilsport Motors, the first place ex-cons stopped to pick up some cheap wheels when they got out of prison. The large lot was located on a busy street in a not-so-nice part of the city. The lot, which bustled with customers and salespeople, was packed with a huge assortment of junkers, muscle cars, old Cadillacs, and Lincoln Continentals—anything an upwardly mobile young pimp would be proud to own. A sign above read: "Repossessed Cars for Sale—CASH ONLY."

As he headed out onto the lot he was approached by another customer who asked "Are these cars really all repossessed?"

"Yeah, somebody else possessed 'em. Now *I* possess 'em."

"Is there any guarantee on them?"

"I guarantee 'em to the gate."

As suggested by this conversation, Samson lacked the diplomatic skills of a salesman, but he made up for this shortcoming with his skill at buying cars on the cheap. He was also a good closer and had a knack for marketing, the key to his success in the business. But Samson didn't expect to remain a used car dealer forever; he had bigger plans. He'd make as much money as possible selling cars, invest his profits, branch out, and build his wealth. He'd already started buying investment properties. Eventually he planned to leverage up, to buy an upscale new car dealership, make a larger fortune in real estate and finance, and when he became super rich, he wanted to get involved in politics, not as a candidate, but as a behind-the-scenes power broker.

Chapter 3
The Last of the Mohicans

"A man's stature is judged by the enemies he makes."
—**Jeremiah Johnson**

"Never give an inch."
—**Ken Kesey**

Samson sat at his desk doing paperwork and smoking a cigar, the sun streaming in through the window. A radio on his desk was broadcasting an NPR report about the Homeland Security Department's purchase of 600 new drone aircraft. "Drone aircraft? I thought those are just for killing terrorists in Pakistan. What the hell does Homeland Security need drones for?" Samson muttered to himself, a question left unanswered by the news report.

A large man entered the office, walking in front of the window, blocking the sunlight, casting a shadow over Samson. His name was Pete Not-so-Happy, a 6-foot 7-inch American Indian, a force of nature, who looked like he'd be a match for Hulk Hogan. In fact, he *had* been a match for Hulk Hogan. He was a former professional wrestler who, years earlier, had gone up against the Hulkster twice. He stood in front of the desk, towering over Samson, waiting for Samson to acknowledge his presence. He wasn't used to being ignored. When he finally realized Samson wasn't going to say anything, Pete announced, "I changed my mind."

"Uh-huh," Samson replied.

"I don't want that pickup."

Samson shrugged his shoulders and continued working, not looking up.

"I made a deposit on it," Pete continued. He waited for a response, but when none came, he added: "Two hundred and fifty dollars."

"Uh-huh."

"I want my money back."

"We don't give money back."

"I want a refund."

"You don't understand. We don't give refunds."

"No, *you* don't understand!" boomed Pete, moving toward Samson, as he banged his huge hand on the desk with enough force to make his point.

Samson finally looked up, and turned off the radio. "What's your name?" he asked quietly, taking a puff on his cigar, apparently unperturbed by the menacing gesture from this humongous Indian.

"Pete Not-So-Happy."

Samson pulled out a file drawer in his desk, dug out Pete's sales contract, stood up, and walked around the desk next to Pete. He pointed to the signature line on the contract. "Is this your signature – Pete Not-So-Happy? Now, you see here where it says 'all deposits nonrefundable?' That means you can't have a refund."

Pete grabbed Samson, lifted him bodily, and threw him against the wall, causing Samson to drop the sales contract.. Samson tried to pull himself together, tucking in his shirt and smoothing his hair, cigar still in his mouth. "Could you wait a second?" he asked.

"What?"

"I don't like to smoke when I'm fighting." Samson put out his cigar in an ashtray on the desk, then slowly turned to stand toe-to- toe with Pete. "Okay, go ahead." He waited for Pete to do something else, but after a moment realized Pete wasn't going to do anything. Pete hadn't expected Samson to stand up to him; smaller guys usually didn't. But Samson hauled back and punched Pete in the stomach with all his might.

Pete didn't flinch. "You shouldn't do that," he said.

"Why?"

"You might make me mad."

"You mean you're not mad already?"

"Not yet."

Pete tried to hit Samson in the face, but Samson, who had been a middleweight boxer on his college team, ducked and Pete's powerful fist went through the wall. Samson again hit Pete in the stomach, with no effect. Pete realized Samson's speed made it difficult to land a punch, so he began moving toward him to back him into the corner, where he could use his mass to take him down.

"Look, this isn't gonna work," Samson said. He pointed out the window to three men who were rushing to his aid. "Those guys work for me; I'm not gonna give the money back." Out the window, his right hand man, Isaac, and two other employees, could be seen rushing toward the office. Isaac, a good looking black man, was carrying a baseball bat. One of the other men carried a monkey wrench, the third man, a crowbar. The three men ran into the office. Pete turned around and retreated. "I'll be back," he said as he headed out the door. It was suddenly as calm as the aftermath of a tornado.

Samson asked Isaac, "Did he mean he'll be back later, or now?"

Isaac was looking out the window, and saw Pete run to his car, and then run back toward the office: "He meant *now*," he said in an urgent tone, as Pete rushed back in.

There he was with a .40 caliber semi-automatic in his hand, which he pointed at close range between Samson's eyes. "Is it worth getting shot over?"

"No, I never like to get shot for two hundred and fifty dollars," Samson said, raising his hands high enough to signal he didn't wish to continue the dispute. "But what about you? Do you really wanna shoot somebody over two hundred and fifty dollars?"

"Look, I came in without a gun. Then your boys ran in here with baseball bats and crowbars. Y'know what I mean?"

"Okay, I see your point. You seem to feel strongly about this. Maybe we could compromise."

"Y'know, I agree with that about compromise," Isaac chimed in. "It's always good when there's a difference of opinion...." Pete turned and pointed the gun at Isaac, who gently put down the baseball bat and also put up his hands, trying unsuccessfully to maintain the continuity of his thought, despite the gun aimed at his head. "Y'know, to, um, uh, I'm just saying...."

As it became clear that Isaac's contribution to the conversation had petered out, Pete turned the gun back toward Samson. "Okay, here's my proposal," Samson said. "I'll give you the money back. You don't shoot me. It's a win-win." Samson kept one hand up, but with the other hand he gingerly reached into his pocket and slowly pulled out a stack of bills. He counted out $250, placed it on the desk, and put the rest of the cash back in his pocket.

Pete kept the gun pointed at Samson, while picking up the money with his free hand. Pete put the money in his jacket pocket, and then waved the gun at the other two employees, who compliantly dropped their weapons. Pete put the gun in his other jacket pocket, and then held out his hand to shake hands with Samson. As Samson and Pete shook hands, Samson looked past Pete, into Isaac's eyes, in a manner which reflected some deep understanding between the two. The other two employees left, but Isaac remained standing, eyeing Pete.

"Thanks," Pete said.

Samson picked up his cigar. "No problem. We always try to keep our customers happy."

As Pete turned to leave and start out the door, Samson signaled to Isaac with a head faint, while at the same time addressing Pete, "Hey, I could use a guy like you," Samson said. "You want a job?" Pete stopped and turned back to face Samson, as Isaac slipped past Pete on his way toward the door. Isaac, now standing behind Pete, reached softly into Pete's jacket pocket and pulled out the $250. Pete, his attention distracted by the question from Samson, didn't notice. Isaac gleefully waved the cash above Pete's head, behind him, showing Samson he got it.

"Doing what?" Pete asked.

• • •

The next morning Pete showed up to start the new job. But there was a little matter that needed to be cleared up first. When he'd gotten home the day before, Pete had discovered the $250 was mysteriously missing from his jacket pocket. Pete confronted Samson, and they nearly got into another fight. Samson didn't admit he'd gotten back the money, but he wanted a man like Pete on his team so he promised Pete a $250 bonus after he repossessed his first five cars. Pete agreed and he went to work.

It didn't take him long to get the hang of it. He was soon driving the "Spoilsport Motors" tow truck into the lot, pulling behind him a car he'd repossessed. Two men ran behind the truck, hollering. "You can't repo my car!" yelled one of the men. The tow truck came to a halt in the lot. The two men ran up to it. One grabbed the door handle and yanked the door open violently, his friend right behind him. "Get outta there, you stupid bastard! I'm gonna kick your ass!" he hollered, clearly an irate customer.

As Pete got out of the truck, he pushed hard on the door, which the man was still holding, throwing the man off balance. When the men saw his size they began to back off. The angry customer looked around desperately as Pete took a step toward him. The customer spotted a tire iron laying on the ground and picked it up. He made a threatening gesture toward Pete while his friend came up behind him. Pete took another step toward them, and the customer tried to hit Pete over the head with the tire iron. But Pete blocked him, grabbing his wrist with one hand, and took the tire iron away from him with the other. Pete bent the tire iron into a horseshoe shape around the customer's neck. The customer and his friend's jaws dropped at this feat of strength, and their threatening demeanor was quickly transformed into obsequious placidity as they backed away.

"Actually, I was thinking of getting rid of that car," the customer said.

"Yeah. He doesn't really want it," his friend agreed. The two men walked away side by side down the street, defeated, the tire iron still around the customer's neck.

Chapter 4
Deliverance

"Every major horror of history was committed in the name of an altruistic motive. Has any act of selfishness ever equaled the carnage perpetrated by disciples of altruism?"
—Ayn Rand

"There are far more things in heaven and on earth, Horatio, than are dreamed of in your philosophies."
—Shakespeare

"Sam, you got another notice from the IRS marked 'urgent.' Do you want me to throw this one away too?" His receptionist stood in the doorway of his office.

"No this time mark it 'deceased' and send it back."

She wrote the word "DECEASED" in large black letters on the envelope from the IRS and placed it in the outgoing mail bin on her desk.

Isaac entered the office and pointed out the window. "Sam, there's a lady here with a car to sell." Samson went to the window and looked out at the car, a noisy old wreck, billowing smoke. Standing next to it was a young woman. She was pregnant and attractive. She was accompanied by two small children who huddled shyly behind her. He was still looking out at the car when the woman came in his office.

"Look, this isn't the Salvation Army," Samson told her brashly, his back still turned. "You could sell it for three hundred dollars to a junk yard."

He could hear her sniffling as if she were crying. "I know. I'm sorry for taking your time." He turned in time to see her and the children start toward the door. She wiped her nose with a handkerchief. "It's all right. I didn't expect…," she said, looking back at him. "I know it isn't worth much."

Samson observed a purple bruise on her face. "Look, I know these are tough times," he said, his tone softened. "What do you need?"

She looked down, seemingly ashamed. "I need to get a bus to my sister's in Colorado, before the baby comes."

"How much will it take?" he asked

"I don't know…six hundred dollars, I think."

Samson took a wad of cash from his pocket, counted out six $100 bills, and handed it to her. She looked at the money, then at him, then back at the money.

Tears of gratitude welled up in her eyes. "I'll never forget this," she said. "Let me find the title for you." Even Samson's eyes teared over, which he tried to conceal with some embarrassment as he went behind his desk and began looking through a desk drawer. She dug through her purse for the title. She held it out to him, but he waived it away. "You'll need the title, won't you?" she asked.

"Keep the car," he replied. "Take it to the junkyard. I'm sure you could use the extra three hundred dollars."

She took his hand in both her hands and looked in his eyes with what seemed to him an almost transcendent glance. "Can I ask you something that's really none of my business?" he asked.

"Is there a connection between the bruise on your face and your urgent need to get to your sister's before the baby comes?"

She let go of his hand and looked down, not answering him.

"Let me guess," he said. "The SOB beat you up, and you want to get away."

She looked up at him briefly, then looked away. "Thanks for your concern, but it's okay. I appreciate what you've done for me—"

"Would it help," he interrupted, "if I beat the crap out of the bastard for you?"

She gave a little smile. "That's very kind of you really, but, well he's in jail now. By the time he gets out, I'll be gone."

"Okay, I didn't mean to butt in. It's just I have a soft spot for pregnant women. My mother was pregnant once—before I was born."

"You have many trials ahead of you, Mr. Samson," she said in a hushed tone. "A terrible darkness is descending on our people, but God will give you the strength to abide and do battle with the oppressors."

Samson, who was something of a cynic, could easily have dismissed this odd prophecy as the raving of a religious zealot. But there was something about the casual yet authoritative tone with which she spoke that made him wonder if there might actually be something to this mysterious warning. Even odder, her words echoed something vaguely biblical Samson's father had said to him on his thirteenth birthday about his destiny. He'd always wondered what it meant, or whether it meant anything at all.

Samson even had a fleeting thought that this incident with the pregnant lady might be some kind of a moral test. Of course he immediately dismissed this thought as idle speculation.

Samson's mind sometimes meandered into such metaphysical musings, but he had enough intellectual discipline to recognize that such speculation about unseen forces of a quasi-religious nature was (a) unproductive, and (b) above his pay grade. Such ruminations didn't lead to actionable insights that were of use to a man of action like Samson.

If the pregnant woman's situation was indeed intended as a moral test to see whether he would do something kind and generous for someone in need, the ramifications were profound and far reaching. It implied that someone, a higher being of some sort, had decided to conduct the test. This in turn implied a level of moral order in the universe which of necessity meant that some higher level of intelligence (presumably God) had (a) organized the whole thing and (b) had decided to target him, Samson, for this particular moral test.

It was unlikely that he would be the only one selected as a subject for such tests, so the further implication of this line of thinking was that God was interested in conducting experiments on human behavior (perhaps analogous to the experiments men do on mice). This suggested to Samson an unlikely degree of intervention in the trivia of human affairs by a Deity, who, if He existed at all, Samson would expect to have better things to do than directly administering such minutia. Arguably, Samson figured, such affairs might be managed by lieutenants, or for that matter, PFCs (privates first class), or other lesser officials in the cosmological hierarchy. Not that Samson explicitly had these thoughts about the incident. As he sensed that these notions were rising up in his consciousness he suppressed them before they could develop. He regarded such unproductive metaphysical speculation as mental masturbation.

He preferred to use his analytical skills to work on more practical problems that could produce useful real world answers, such as, what is the level national debt as a percentage of GDP has to reach before, based on historical economic data, the debt burden of the nation irreversibly leads to the collapse of the currency, as a result of which financial ruin, hyperinflation, social chaos, rioting, massive starvation, and usually, the violent overthrow of the government inevitably ensues? (Author's note: There is, by the way, a definitive numerical answer to this question, which isn't provided here. However, here's a hint: Unless Congress cuts federal spending this year by $1.2 trillion, the United States will reach that point of financial no return, and consequent national disintegration and worldwide economic Armageddon, in eleven days. That's not eleven days from the day this was written; it's eleven days from the day you read it. Mark your calendar.)

"I didn't expect you to be generous," the pregnant lady continued. "They said you're greedy."

"They're right; I *am* greedy," he answered, wondering who *they* were.

"But you have a good heart," she said.

"Well, keep it under your hat. I don't wanna ruin my reputation."

When she left, Isaac made a derisive comment about Samson not buying her junker. "No," Samson replied, "I didn't buy it."

That afternoon it all started.

Chapter 5
The Philistines

"My whole life the government has been my enemy. When it has not been trying to rob me it has been trying to silence me. I have never had any contact with it that was not an assault on my security, and an affront to my dignity.
—**H. L. Mencken**

"There's one way to find out if a man is honest: ask him; if he says yes, you know he is crooked."
—**Mark Twain**

"Sam, that guy Phil S. Stein from the Justice Department is here again," the receptionist announced over the intercom.

"Tell him I'm in a meeting," Samson told her.

Phil S. Stein was standing in the reception area and heard this conversation, so he brushed past the receptionist and walked into Samson's office.

"Are you busy, Mr. Samson?" he asked.

Samson was sitting with his feet up on his desk, reading the newspaper, and smoking a cigar. "Yeah, I'm busy," he said.

Stein, an officious bureaucrat with an abrasive personality, stood in front of Samson's desk, hat in hand. "Well, what's a good time for you?"

"A couple of blondes in a hot tub," Samson quipped, still not looking up from his newspaper.

Stein was a government official and had no sense of humor. This response just irritated him. He became more assertive. "You need to answer some questions," he said. He sat down, put his hat on Samson's desk, and then put his feet up on the desk, as if to convey he could pretty much do what he wanted. "As you know, we're investigating the complaint of your customer Lisa Pressman that the car you sold her broke down after a week."

"Yeah, so what?" Samson replied.

"So you think you can just sell people cars that don't run?"

"It did run."

"A week later it stopped running."

"Yeah, used cars do that sometimes."

"So that's a breach of warranty."

"A breach of warranty, huh. Tell me something," Samson said, finally putting down the newspaper, and looking at his adversary. "To have a breach of warranty, there has to be a warranty, right?"

"Well, uh—"

"So there was no warranty. Hence, there couldn't have been a breach of warranty. Get it? You went to law school, right?"

"Of course, but that—"

"So how is it you don't know this?" Samson interrupted.

"Because you're wrong," Stein shot back. "Even if there's no warranty, there can be a breach of warranty. It's called an implied warranty of merchantability. See, I learned that in law school."

"Implied warranty on used cars? I don't think so."

"What you think doesn't matter. What matters is what *I* think."

"Really? Why's that?"

"'Cause I'm the government. And if I say there's a warranty, that means there's a warranty."

"Yeah, but we sell all cars 'as is.' That means there *is* no warranty. I told her that."

"How do I know you're not lying?" Stein asked.

"Look, I don't always tell the truth, but I never lie," Samson replied.

"You just lied about being in a meeting."

"I didn't lie; I told my secretary to lie."

"I don't like your attitude," Stein said. "And what about the truth-in-lending disclosure?"

"What *about* the truth-in-lending disclosure?" Samson responded, with no less of an attitude.

"You financed the purchase of the car, right?"

"Yeah, I financed it. So what?"

"So if you financed it, you're required by law to make the truth-in-lending disclosure to the customer" Stein explained.

"So what's your point?" Samson asked.

"My point is," said Stein, "that in your response to our inquiry regarding this matter, you made no mention of having made the truth-in-lending disclosures to Ms. Pressman. Therefore, I have to assume that you failed to make these disclosures, which is a violation of federal law."

"Let me get this straight," Samson shot back. "It's illegal not to make the truth-in-lending disclosures. I didn't say I made them, so you *assumed* I didn't make them, correct?"

"Correct."

"So it's also illegal to steal wallets," Samson continued. "I made no mention of not stealing her wallet. So did you also assume that I *did* steal her wallet?"

Stein picked up a stapler from Samson's desk and began fidgeting with it nervously, repeatedly opening and closing the clip that held the staples. Samson watched him with visible irritation. "Can I ask you a question?" Samson said. "Why is the U.S. Attorney's office suddenly so interested in the business of a local used-car dealer? Don't you have bigger fish to fry?"

"Yeah, I have bigger fish to fry. And smaller fish to fry. We fry fish of all sizes now. Were you under the impression, sir, that there are limits on our domain? Limitations on our power? You're living in a dream world, Mr. Samson. Things have changed and your dream will soon be over."

"Yeah, that's great. Are we done now?"

"Not yet." Stein tried a different tack: "Do you have health insurance?"

"Health insurance?"

"Yeah."

"None of your business."

"Oh, that's where you're wrong, Mr. Samson. Under the Affordable Healthcare Act of 2010, it *is* my business!"

Although you'd never guess it to look at him as he wheeled and dealed in his car lot, Sam Samson had an Ivy League education—well, after a fashion. He had dropped out of Cornell after his junior year. But he'd been in college long enough to learn the basics. He knew that ontogeny recapitulates phylogeny and understood the difference between the Hegelian dialectic and dialectic materialism (Marx's perversion of the dialectic). He understood the distinction between epistemology and teleology, was familiar with Kant's categorical imperative, had mastered the law of supply and demand, and knew that profit is maximized at the point on the graph where marginal revenue equals marginal cost. He had written a paper on the Federalist Papers (for which he got an A+), understood the third law of thermodynamics and the Heisenberg Uncertainty Principle, and had a passing familiarity with Einstein's Theory of Relativity. He even knew what stereospecific autocatalysis is. He'd been, as Dylan put it, "through all of F. Scott Fitzgerald's books," and "was very well read, it's well known." He could competently exchange abstract ideas and word monger, and had he chosen to, he could have hung out with New York literary intellectuals or Harvard academicians and gotten by passably well at their cocktail parties.

But Samson felt like he didn't fit in that world, the easy explanation being that he had been a working class boy on an athletic scholarship at an elite university. He was a good enough student that he could have qualified for an academic scholarship. Or maybe it was because he got into drugs his junior year and lost interest in his studies. But it really went deeper than that. The truth is he didn't quite fit in anywhere. He was a born iconoclast. No one taught him to be a wise ass; it was his nature from birth. He was arrogant, and took pleasure in showing contempt for either pretension or stupidity. He made enemies easily, but it didn't bother him. Seeing people get pissed off over trivia that wasn't worth getting pissed off about amused him. He had no compunction about letting people know he was smart, and if they had a problem with that, he didn't give a shit.

Stupidity in and of itself didn't bother Samson. He understood everyone was born with different talents, and if people were stupid in a private way that didn't affect him, he was tolerant of it. It was when other people's stupidity negatively impacted his life that he became irritated, such as planning board or DMV officials oblivious to the misery their petty little rules have on the lives of real people. Or, for that matter, any government official who was imposing some annoying regulation on him with no rational nexus to any social good or anything remotely resembling a cost benefit analysis. It didn't bother him when stupid people worked in the private sector because you had a choice whether to deal with them. But he felt stupid people should be barred from elective office, barred from working for government agencies, kept off school boards, and banned by law from the public sector. And if barring stupid people from public office meant decimating the ranks of Congress, he was okay with that.

It wasn't stupidity per se that bothered Samson, but the combination of stupidity and power. He suffered not fools gladly. He had little patience for a world in which people who were dumber than he was, petty tyrants who sought to fill the void in their desperate, meaningless lives, by lording it over the rest of us, had the power to make stupid rules that he was expected to obey. And that's why he heard himself saying to Phil S. Stein, "Kiss my ass." Diplomacy was not Samson's strong suit.

"Excuse me?" Stein replied.

Louder, Samson repeated, "I said kiss my ass."

• • •

Stein was surprised at the gratuitous insult, yet his eyes were somehow strangely vacant. He was not accustomed to being commanded to kiss the ass of people he was investigating. Usually his targets were obsequious. They were afraid of him, well, not of him, but of the power he wielded. He knew his position at the agency conferred on him the power to make life miserable for small businessmen like Samson, or even put them out of business. There was no way that he, Phil S. Stein, was going to take shit from this obnoxious, self-important, abrasive, sleazebag used car dealer, who had such a high opinion of himself even though he was nothing more than a slimy little dirt bag petty-ante wheeler dealer who made his living off the backs of working people by conning them into buying junker cars at inflated prices with financing packages they couldn't afford.

Samson stood up, walked around to Stein's side of the desk, took the stapler out of Stein's hands, pushed the clip back in, and placed the stapler back on the desk, next to Stein's hat. Then he walked over to the door and opened it, as if inviting Stein to leave. "Don't you have some mobsters you could investigate?" he asked.

Stein stood up and picked up his hat, in the process "accidentally" knocking the stapler onto the floor. Pretending not to notice, he put on his hat and turned toward the door.

"I'm not done with you," he said as he walked out. Samson shut the door behind him, not exactly slamming it, but with more force than was necessary to close it.

Chapter 6
The Sting

"Every revolution evaporates and leaves behind only the slime of a new bureaucracy."
—Franz Kafka

*"You said you'd never compromise with the mystery tramp,
but now you realize
He's not selling any alibis,
as you stare into the vacuum of his eyes
And ask him do you want to make a deal?"*
—Bob Dylan

Phil S. Stein sat at his desk in the local office of the Justice Department, talking on the phone. "Deceased? I was just out there. Sam Samson's not deceased. He sells more junkers than McDonald's sells hamburgers."

At the other end of the line, IRS Special Agent Elliott Mess spoke into the phone in a husky whisper, almost conspiratorial in tone. "Is he in compliance with the tax code?"

"No way. I wanna nail the arrogant SOB," Stein answered.

"Under the new Plan for Universal Compliance," Mess responded, "that shouldn't be difficult. He fits the profile of a first-line target. We'll send in an undercover agent."

"Good, let's do it. He likes money. Let's see if we can entrap him in a drug deal."

Not long after this conversation, a stereotypical drug dealer—complete with slicked back black hair, a gold chain around his neck, an open collar, a large earring in one ear, and wearing a fancy suit—sat across from Samson at his desk. Pete happened to be standing in the office when the drug dealer came in, and out of curiosity he stayed on, listening in on the conversation.

"I'm looking for capital," the dealer explained. "I get the stuff for seven hundred and fifty thousand. It has a street value of three and a half million. I already have four hundred and fifty thousand. So you put up three hundred thousand. You get back six hundred thousand cash two days later."

"How do I know I'll get the money back?" Samson asked.

"You don't trust me?" asked the dealer. Samson stared at him incredulously. "Okay, you can stay with me the whole time. You can even bring your big Indian with you."

"What do you think, Pete?" Samson looked over at Pete. But Pete stared straight ahead, his arms folded, and didn't answer. Samson looked back to the drug dealer. "I don't think he likes the deal."

"I don't care what *he* likes. What about you?"

"I don't like it either."

"What don't you like about it?"

"I don't like drugs. And I don't like drug-dealing scum bags," Samson said.

"I thought you like money."

"I don't like it *that* much. So why don't you get your slick ass outta here?"

Samson stood up, signaling the conversation was done.

The drug dealer took his time getting to his feet. "You think you're a hotshot, don't you, Samson? You could learn something from me."

"I already *know* how to be an asshole."

The drug dealer came up to Samson in a subdued, yet menacing manner. Samson didn't flinch. Pete, his arms still crossed, didn't budge, but his eyes were fixated on the dealer.

"You might run into some bad luck," said the dealer in a menacing tone.

"Yeah, that's what I keep hearing."

The drug dealer walked out, slamming the door behind him.

. . .

Phil S. Stein was disappointed to learn that Samson didn't take the bait on the drug deal. "Let's go to plan B," he said into the phone to Elliott Mess. "Who's available?"

"Delilah," Mess said.

"Ooh. Delilah. Perfect! She always gets her man."

"We'll send her over there to buy a car," Mess said.

The Old Testament, Samson and Delilah:

Samson fell in love with a woman in the Valley of Sorek whose name was Delilah. The rulers of the Philistines [the enemies of Israel] went to her and said, "See if you can lure him into showing you the secret of his great strength and how we can overpower him so we may tie him up and subdue him. Each one of us will give you eleven hundred shekels of silver." —Judges 16

Chapter 7
Poison Ivy

"We learn from experience that men never learn anything from experience."
—**George Bernard Shaw**

"She comes on like a rose, but everybody knows, you'll be scratching like a hound – the minute you start to mess around..."
—**The Coasters**

Delilah, the ultimate weapon in the IRS undercover arsenal, entered the Spoilsport Motors' lot. She was dressed revealingly, slightly sexier than the average Fox News reporterette—not in bad taste, but still managing to exude sex appeal. Appearances to the contrary, she was no bimbo. She walked up and down the lot once and took a quick look at a couple of cars, but didn't bother to open the doors. She found the one she wanted, went into Sam Samson's office, and stood in his doorway.

Samson looked up. He stared and cleared his throat. "Who are *you*?"

"I'm fine; who are *you*?" she shot back.

"I'm fine too. What can you do for me?"

"I can buy that old Thunderbird."

"Have you taken it for a test drive?"

"It runs, doesn't it?"

"Yeah."

"I don't need a test drive; I want it.

"I'd like to take *you* for a test drive."

"You can take *me* for a test drive after I buy the car. I'll give you five thousand for it."

"The price is *eight* thousand."

"I'll give you five thousand for it."

He took the bait. "I'll let you have it for five thousand on two conditions: Pay cash and go out to dinner with me tonight."

"Can I trust you?"

"Yeah," he said. "I'm very honest. I never cheat anybody out of less than fifty-thousand dollars."

Delilah took the cash out of her purse. Samson stood up. She came behind the desk and stood close to him, her lips so close to his that they were practically kissing. She looked into his eyes, her breasts lightly brushing up against his solar plexus, and stuffed the cash slowly into his pants pocket.

Samson, with some difficulty, disengaged from Delilah, and sat at the desk. Delilah sat opposite him, her legs crossed, leaning forward, moving one leg back and forth sensually, while he wrote out the sales form. "What's your name?" he asked.

"Delilah. What's your name?"

"Samson. What's your last name?"

"I don't have a last name. What's *your* last name?"

"Samson."

"Your name's Samson Samson?"

"Sam Samson. But you can call me Samson."

That night, Samson and Delilah went out to dinner as agreed. You may be wondering whether Samson wasn't being naive in allowing himself to be taken in by this femme fatale IRS undercover agent. Samson had been around the block and was no fool when it came to women. However, like most guys, he suffered from the diminished intellectual capacity, sometimes referred to as the estrogen effect (and sometimes referred to by the cruder colloquial expression "thinking with his dick"), which occurs when the presence of attractive females causes the male's blood to flow in the opposite direction from the brain. This is a physiological reaction and there's little that members of the male gender can do about it, short of going to live in a monastery.

Samson had been through a womanizing phase as a young man. But he wasn't interested in one-night stands anymore, although he occasionally succumbed to temptation. His reaction to this bombshell who had come so suddenly into his life was ambivalent. He had good instincts, and he sensed that it was coming too easily. But he was also irresistibly attracted to her, and from that first repartee in the car lot that afternoon, he knew she wasn't just a hottie; she was also a kindred spirit. However, he also sensed, notwithstanding the fog from the estrogen effect, that he needed to keep his guard up. But he was willing to take the risk, and was confident, incorrectly as it turned out, he could handle whatever was coming his way.

As they sat in a fancy restaurant waiting for dinner, Delilah asked him, "Are you rich, Samson?" That may have sounded like an odd question coming from an undercover agent, who presumably wanted to gain the target's trust, but Delilah didn't follow the rules. She instinctively knew that the best way to get close to Samson was to be herself, with no pretense. She sensed he'd respect her directness. Girls naturally want to know if the guy is rich, but how many have the chutzpah to come out and ask? She was making no effort to conceal who she was, which was ironic, because the entire enterprise was a concealment of who she was. Somehow, coming from her, the brazen question seemed spontaneous and almost innocent.

Still, Samson was surprised, so he ignored the question and changed the subject. "This meal better be good," he said. "It already cost me three thousand dollars," referring to the reduced price on the Thunderbird.

Delilah moved her chair closer to his. "You'll get your money's worth, Sam," she said. Then she quickly returned to the topic. "So *are* you?"

"Am I what?"

"Rich."

"Yeah. Why?"

"I like rich men."

"What is it you like about them?"

"Their money."

"You're not gonna *get* my money."

"I didn't say I was gonna get your money."

"Y'know, Delilah, because I'm a single guy I drive a snazzy car to attract girls. So what kind of girls do you think I attract? The kind who like guys who drive snazzy cars."

"So get rid of the snazzy car."

"I will, when I find a girl who doesn't care about snazzy cars. But my point is it's the same thing with the money. I don't usually brag about how rich I am on the first date."

"What, you wait 'til the second date?"

"Yeah, cause most girls wait 'til the second date to ask if I'm rich. But the question I have to ask myself, if a woman likes me because I have money is how long will she stick around if I lose the money?"

"So don't lose the money."

"Y'know, I used to be into *stuff*," he said. "The new Cadillac, the stereo, the Harley, the boat. Then, I met an extraordinary man who taught me I can live without all those material possessions."

"And who was that?"

"My ex-wife's lawyer."

"Oh. Very spiritual dude, huh? So how'd you get rich?"

"I buy low, sell high, deal in cash."

"So you won't have to report it?"

• • •

Samson looked at her for a moment, letting the question hang in the air. *Here's a woman*, he thought, *who I just met, and she's asking me, in effect, if I'm a felon.* Tax evasion is an odd felony. It's the only crime where you go to jail, not for taking other peoples' money, but for trying to keep other people from taking *your* money. And it's as commonplace as traffic infractions, so people talk about it openly. But Samson regarded this as a mistake. You wouldn't tell a stranger that you robbed banks. So why admit to evading taxes. Samson changed the subject.

"Let's talk about someone else," he said.

"Okay, like who?" she asked.

"Well, what about you?"

"I don't talk about myself."

"What do you do?"

"I'm a consultant."

"A consultant, huh. Usually when people tell me they're a consultant, it means they're unemployed."

"Okay, I'm unemployed. I'm an unemployed consultant."

"Do you want a job?"

"Sure."

"What are your skills?

"I'm sexy."

"Yeah, I noticed that."

"And I have a good personality."

"I noticed that too."

"And I'm good in bed."

"All right, you got the job."

"But that doesn't mean you can treat me like a sex object."

"You don't want me to treat you like a sex object?"

"No."

"All right then make sure you don't act like a sex object."

"Are you accusing me of acting like a sex object?"

"No, that's not—you're the one who brought it up!"

"You're so sexist!"

"Yeah, I may be sexist, so what? Maybe that's why you like me."

"Who says I like you?"

"You know why men treat women like sex objects?"

"No, why?"

"Because women *are* sex objects. And do you know which women object to men treating women like sex objects? "

"Let me guess…"

"The ones who men *don't* treat as sex objects." he interrupted. "It's unattractive women who complain, not that men are treating *them* as sex objects, but that men are treating *other* women as sex objects. Women *like* being treated as sex objects."

"Okay, but not while I'm working."

"How about when you're not working?"

"We'll see."

Samson and Delilah didn't have sex that night. Samson knew one-night stands only lasted one night, and he wanted this to last longer.

• • •

Delilah was in no rush either. She had long ago figured out that guys can't tell the difference between being in love and being horny. She knew her job would be easier if Samson fell for her. But she was also trying to figure out how to resolve the conflict between her professional duty to take him down for the government, and her personal attraction to him. Although Delilah wasn't above using her feminine wiles in her work, she didn't consider it her job to have sex with targets. She'd made that mistake once before, and she'd regretted it.

She'd told Samson that what she liked about rich men was their money, but it really went deeper. True, she liked money, but even more than the money she liked the men who make money. In Darwinian terms, this could be seen as an atavistic throwback to prehistoric times, when, based on natural selection, and survival of the fittest, women were naturally attracted to strong men, great hunters and warriors, who could provide amply through the long winter for their mates and offspring, and fend off with spears any would-be attackers. There's nothing immoral or shallow about women's instinctive biological attraction to men who have the means to be good providers. That's why movie stars, rock stars, and athletes don't have trouble getting a date. She saw Samson as tough, smart, self-confident, and good looking to boot. This was an interesting assignment.

• • •

It wasn't until the fifth time they saw each other that they became physically intimate. It was a warm, humid, summer night. Delilah was at Samson's place, a well-furnished modern home with a swimming pool and hot tub in the backyard. They swam and found themselves making out, first in the pool then in the hot tub. It got pretty steamy, and he said he'd give her a hot oil massage, using a bottle of sesame oil which he'd already warmed up in the kitchen. He told her, in all sincerity, that he just wanted her to relax and enjoy the massage and didn't think they should have sex. It culminated, of course, with fabulous sex. *What a great ploy*, he thought, *to get a girl to have sex by saying we shouldn't have sex.*

When it was over, she said, "That was amazing."

"Was it a religious experience?"

"No, an orgasm."

They lay there on their backs for a few moments staring up at the stars, and then she said, "Sam, there's something I should tell you."

"Don't bother; I know."

"What?"

"I'm drawn to you like a moth to the flame. I know what happens when you play with fire."

This consummation of their relationship under the stars occurred eight days after Delilah had begun working at Spoilsport Motors. Samson had her doing both office work and sales. She said she was good at bookkeeping, so her first day on the job Samson asked her to assist with accounting. He introduced her to his accountant, a Vietnamese guy named Buddha. "Keep an eye on Buddha," Samson said. "He's very devious with a computer, as First National Bank can attest."

"Why, what did you do?" Delilah asked Buddha.

"Three and a half years."

"For embezzlement?"

"Yeah, and bank fraud."

"How much did you get?"

"More than twelve million, but I had to give it back."

Buddha was underemployed at Spoilsport Motors. His parents were Vietnamese immigrants, but he had been born in the United States. He was a math prodigy, got 800 on his math SATs, and had been a computer science major at Stanford. While still a student he played a key role in launching two major Internet sites which later went public and made billions for their founders, but not for Buddha. He was a Mark Zuckerberg–type genius who didn't care much about money; he got a kick out of doing things on the net that not many people could do.

After college he was a partner in an Internet consulting firm that contracted with banks on matters of cyber security. That's how he got in trouble. When he got caught with the $12 million he appropriated from the bank, his defense was that he had only taken the money to demonstrate a weakness in the bank's security so he could figure out how to fix it. He said he intended to give the money back. The jury didn't believe him.

One of his parole conditions was that he couldn't work online, which was why he was doing accounting at Spoilsport Motors.

• • •

On her second day on the job Delilah managed to stay late at the office. After everyone else left, she worked furtively at Buddha's computer, printing out accounting files, and sending emails to her contact at the IRS, Elliott Mess, indirectly through a separate email account which had been set up for this purpose. Then she deleted the emails from the Spoilsport Motors Computer, making it unlikely anyone there would discover them. She knew the information she was gathering was enough to ruin Sam Samson. For the first time in her career she felt a sensation that was somewhat unfamiliar: guilt. But it was too late to turn back. The Rubicon had been crossed; the die was cast.

The Old Testament:

Delilah said to Samson, "Tell me the secret of your great strength and how you can be tied up and subdued."... "No razor has ever been used on my head," he said, ... "If my head were shaved, my strength would leave me, and I would become as weak as any other man."... After putting him to sleep on her lap, she called for someone to shave off the seven braids of his hair, and so began to subdue him.[c] And his strength left him. He awoke from his sleep.... But he did not know that the LORD had left him. Then the Philistines seized him, gouged out his eyes and took him down to Gaza.—Judges 16

Chapter 8

The Taxman Cometh

"Come let us reason together. ....But if ye refuse and rebel, ye shall be devoured with the sword."
—Isaiah 1:18

*"You never give me your money.
You only give me your funny paper.
And in the middle of negotiation you break down."*
—The Beatles

Six days later, on a Sunday afternoon, after Delilah had spent the night at Samson's, he sat in a chair in his bathroom, looking in the mirror, a sheet covering him, Delilah standing behind him with a scissors. She'd been bugging him about how long his hair was getting, and he'd agreed to let her give him a haircut. Samson noticed that she kept looking at her watch nervously, as if expecting someone. As she finished the haircut, Samson felt weak, as if he might be coming down with something. The doorbell rang. Samson threw off the sheet and went downstairs to the front door. Delilah stayed upstairs.

Samson opened the door. It was a gloomy, gray day. There, dripping wet from a downpour, stood somber, stone-faced Special Agent Elliott Mess and a younger agent, his sidekick. Samson immediately got a bad feeling seeing this guy on his porch, in black and white, dressed in a 1930s three-piece suit, trench coat, and fedora hat.

"Mr. Sam Samson?" Mess asked.

"Yes?

"Elliott Mess, Special Agent, Internal Revenue."

"Elliott Ness? From 'The Untouchables'?"

"No. Not *'Ness.' Mess!* Elliott Mess."

"You gotta be kidding."

"I don't kid."

As he said this, Mess shoved his badge up to Samson's nose. The agents started to push past Samson into the house. Samson could swear he heard the 1960s "Untouchables" theme song, seeming to come from out of nowhere. "Excuse me," Samson protested, standing in their way. "I didn't invite you in. Do you have a warrant?"

"We have something better than a warrant, Mr. Samson. We have tax liens on everything you own," Mess said. He handed Samson several official-looking pieces of paper. "Now, it's your choice. We can either have a conversation, or we can go ahead and execute the liens." Samson stood down as they brushed past him into his entry way. Mess and the other agent shook off the rain, as Samson closed the door. Samson's eyes went back and forth suspiciously between the two agents. He stood alert, in the pose of someone whose space had been invaded, as if an attack might be imminent. The agents were looking around, making mental notes about the home, and its contents, the obvious evidence of opulence that was naturally of interest to IRS agents.

"The IRS has sent you several notices," Mess began, "and received no response. The last one came back marked 'deceased.' Are you deceased, Mr. Samson?"

"Well, I was. But actually, I've been feeling better."

Mess took out a notepad and duly noted this response. "Mr. Samson," he asked, "how do you manage to live in an eight-hundred-thousand-dollar house, when, according to the only tax return you've ever filed, you only make fourteen thousand dollars a year?" Mess waited for a moment, but seeing no response, he continued, "How do you have money for groceries?"

Samson paused, then cleared his throat. "I have a garden," he said.

Mess also noted this response on his pad. "Apparently you are unaware, Mr. Samson. The 'gardening loophole' has been closed by the Tax Reform Act of 2009. Under the new code those with gardens are required to have their broccoli and spinach appraised. You have to report the fair market value of all produce as taxable income."

"Hey, I'm honest, but poor," Samson replied.

"Well, you're about to get a lot poorer."

"How much you figure I owe?"

The agents were prepared for this question. Mess's sidekick took out a calculator from his coat pocket and handed it to Mess, who began pushing buttons on it. "Let's see. You reported no income from 1993 to 2011. Assuming annual taxable income of two hundred eighty-six thousand, that would place you in the 39.6 percent marginal bracket, with compound interest at nine percent, plus accrued penalties you now owe..." Mess punched the numbers into the calculator "...two million four hundred seventy-eight thousand five hundred and twenty-nine dollars and forty-two cents." Mess tore off the print-out from the calculator and handed it to Samson. Samson crumpled up the print-out and threw it on the floor. Then he reached into his back pocket, pulled out his wallet, removed a stack of bills, and started counting.

"Uh…was that two million four hundred uh…?" Samson fumbled with the money, recounting it. "Gee, um, I don't have that much." He held out the contents of his wallet, $322, to Mess, but Mess didn't take it. So Samson put his wallet back in his pocket and casually put his hands in his pockets. Mess stared at him icily, irritated that he didn't seem to be taking this seriously.

"What happens if I don't give it to you?" Samson asked.

"We got it from Al Capone, Mr. Samson. We can get it from *you*."

"Yeah, I heard about the Al Capone thing. Okay, fine, I'll write you a check."

Samson went from the entry way into the living room. The agents followed him in. He sat down at his desk and removed the checkbook from the drawer, the agents standing above him casting a shadow over him.

"How much did you say that was?"

"Two million four hundred seventy-eight thousand five hundred and twenty-nine dollars and forty-two cents," the younger agent said.

Samson started to write the check but, looking at his check register he hesitated. At the same time Mess was looking at some data on his cell phone. "Don't bother," Mess said. "You only have twenty-two-hundred dollars in your personal checking account."

"How do you know that?" Samson asked.

"It's my job to know."

"No, but I mean, how can you get access to that information?"

"The Bank Secrecy Act of 1970 gives me access."

Samson put down the pen, and turned back to face the agents. "Well, then I guess we have a problem. If there's only twenty two hundred dollars in my account, I guess I can't pay it."

"No, *we* don't have a problem, Mr. Samson," Mess said. "*You* have a problem. We can go to Plan B."

"Plan B?"

"We've already done a rough appraisal of your assets." Mess dialed some numbers on his smart phone. A bunch of data came up on his screen. "Let's see," he continued, "yesterday your brokerage account closed with a portfolio value of three hundred eighty-five thousand two hundred twenty-two dollars. According to information we obtained yesterday under the Act, your company bank account has more than twenty-five thousand dollars in it. You have three rental properties, which, according to online valuation at Zillow.com, cross-referenced with your bank mortgages, have approximately six hundred ten thousand in equity between them. According to DMV records, which have been corroborated by satellite photos taken this morning at 7:45 a.m., you have seventy-two vehicles in your car lot. Get the picture? Between your home, rental properties, business assets, vehicles, and stock market accounts, there should be enough to cover it."

"But that would leave me broke."

"That's not really my problem, is it?"

Samson leaned back casually in his chair, and put his hands behind his head, looking like he was deep in thought. "Let me ask you a question. You guys interested in making a deal?"

Samson looked back and forth between the two agents, who stood quiet for a moment, not sure what to make of this unusual proposal.

"What kind of deal?" Mess asked.

"Well, let's say I were to pay you in cash."

"How much cash?" the younger agent asked.

"Say, a hundred-fifty-thousand dollars cash."

Mess took the other agent by the elbow and led him back into the hallway for a private discussion. Samson could hear their muffled voices arguing, but couldn't make out what they were saying. They returned to the living room.

"Not enough," Mess said.

"How much is enough?"

"Four hundred thousand."

"Four-hundred-thousand dollars cash? Are you crazy?"

"No problem. We'll go to plan B." The agents turned to go and headed toward the entry way, but Samson called them back.

"Wait, I want to work with you guys, but you have to be realistic. I don't have half that much."

"Tell you what. Pay us right now, and we'll take less." Mess looked at his watch as if he were in a hurry. So few hours in the day, so many taxpayers to intimidate.

"How much less?" Samson asked.

"Two hundred thousand. Cash. Nonnegotiable."

The other agent looked at Mess in confusion, appalled that he was coming down so much. Mess whispered something in his ear.

"And if I give you two hundred thousand that'll be it?" Samson asked.

"Yeah, that'll be it."

"We'll call it even and you'll leave me alone, right?"

"Right, we'll leave you alone."

Now you may wonder why Samson, a man who clearly didn't like to part with money, would be willing to pay $200,000. But he figured he didn't have much choice. It was that or lose everything, so by comparison he thought he was getting off cheap. Samson got up, crossed the room, turned down a hallway, opened a door, and went down into the basement. The agents started snooping through Samson's desk drawers and rifling through papers. They heard him coming up the steps, and moved away from the desk.

Samson returned, carrying a large brown paper bag. He saw that a desk drawer had been left open and closed it.

"Look," Samson said. "Here's the deal. I want a receipt, signed by both of you, showing payment in full satisfaction of all taxes owed."

Mess and the other agent exchanged glances, confirming they were on the same page.

Mess nodded. "Write it up."

Samson sat down at his desk, typed out a receipt on his computer, printed it, and handed it to Mess. Mess signed it and handed it to the other agent, who also signed it, and handed it back to Mess. Samson eyed the receipt in Mess's hand, as Mess eyed the brown bag on Samson's desk. Samson put his hand to his chin as if contemplating how to handle the exchange. He pointed to a coffee table. Mess placed the receipt on the table, still eyeing the bag. Samson turned the bag over and dumped a huge pile of $100 bills on the table. The agents stared at the cash.

"You keep two hundred thousand in cash in your basement?" asked the younger agent.

Samson shrugged his shoulders. "For emergencies," he said.

"You said you're poor," Mess said.

"Hey, rich or poor, it's good to have lots of cash."

The agents began counting the money as Samson picked up the receipt, folded it and placed it in his shirt pocket. Then he sat down on the couch, put his feet up on the table on which they were counting, lit his cigar, and began reading a magazine. They finished counting and stuffed the cash in their pockets, which bulged with the money.

"Did I say two hundred thousand?" Mess said. "I meant *three* hundred thousand."

Samson put down the magazine and looked up. "*Three* hundred thousand."

"Yeah."

Samson's eyes went back and forth between the two agents, as he sized up the situation. He patted the shirt pocket where the receipt was, making sure it was still there. He stood slowly, preparing to confront this apparent shakedown, his hands at his sides. The three of them stood there for a dramatic moment, looking in each other's faces in a manner reminiscent of the famous gun battle scene from *The Good, The Bad, and The Ugly* where Clint Eastwood, Lee Van Cleaf, and Eli Wallach stared each other down before they drew in the final showdown. The theme song from *The Good, the Bad, and the Ugly* played in the background. Samson was standing with his back toward the wall, effectively cornered by the two agents.

Mess stepped toward Samson and held out his hand. "Give me the receipt back," he commanded.

"Okay, give me the money back," Samson replied. He took a puff on his cigar, holding the smoke in his mouth.

"We don't give money back."

Samson blew out the smoke in Mess's face. "I don't give *receipts* back," he said.

The two agents looked at each other and then jumped in unison toward Samson. They tackled him at the same time, one hitting high, the other low, knocking him back onto the couch. While the other agent held down his body Mess choked him. Samson fought back fiercely, pushing Mess's face, and kicking both of them in the legs, but the other agent managed to get the receipt out of his pocket and hand it to Mess, who put it in his own pants pocket. Mess punched Samson in the jaw, and the two agents hastily made for the entry way. Samson, staggering from the blow, pulled himself up and followed them. Delilah had heard the commotion and come down the stairway. Mess got to the front door and took hold of the door knob. Samson grabbed his shoulder from behind. "Either give me my money back or give me the receipt!"

"I'll give you a receipt!" Mess said, as he pulled free from Samson's grasp, wheeled around and punched him in the eye, knocking him over. Mess tried to pull the door open, but Samson kneeled in front of it, blocking it. As Samson got up, wobbly and still on one knee, he punched Mess in the groin with an uppercut, doubling him over. Delilah, who was now in the entry way, went to Mess's aid. She pulled a gun from her purse, and stood over Samson, pointing it at him. The other agent also pulled his gun and fired a warning shot which passed in front of Samson's face, cutting off the tip of his cigar, and shattering the large window which adjoined his front door. He didn't really want to shoot Samson, because he knew if there were a shooting he'd have some "splaining" to do. But he shoved the gun into Samson's face. Samson was still on one knee. The agent pushed the gun forward, pressing it against Samson's face, physically forcing him onto his back, the damaged cigar still in his mouth.

Mess, recovering from the blow to his groin, managed to stand up straight, towering over Samson, who now had a black eye. Mess pulled his gun also. The other agent, seeing the situation was under control, re-holstered his gun, and went outside to start the car. Mess, standing shoulder to shoulder with Delilah, pointed his gun down at Samson's face, put his foot on Samson's chest, and looked down at him. "You aren't too smart, are you?" he said.

Mess raised his foot, like he was going to stomp on Samson's stomach. But Delilah held him back with her hand. "I can't do this, Elliott," she said. She put her gun back in her purse and went out, leaving the door open.

Mess backed out through the doorway, his gun still pointing at Samson, and then backed his way toward the car. Samson pulled himself up, stood in the doorway, and watched Mess and Delilah rushing to their car in the rain. Before getting in, Mess shot out the windshield of Samson's Corvette, parked in the driveway. "I don't like that guy," Samson said to himself out loud. He put the broken cigar back in his mouth and re-lit it, as he watched them drive off.

Chapter 9
Through the Looking Glass

"He has erected a multitude of new offices, and sent hither swarms of officers to harass our people and eat out their substance."
—Declaration of Independence

"'Curiouser and curiouser!' cried Alice."
—Lewis Carroll

Samson went to bed that night with a headache. He slept poorly and had restless dreams. He slept in the next morning and thought he'd go into work late. When he got out of bed, late in the morning, still half asleep, he looked in the mirror and saw his black eye, which had gotten blacker overnight. The vivid memory of the day before came rushing back.

Even more disturbing than getting robbed and beaten up by IRS agents, was the sudden shock of discovering that Delilah was one of them. His conversation with Delilah over dinner on their first date now made sense on an entirely different level. Of course she likes rich men; it's her job to take their money. But he couldn't afford to dwell on the depressing truth that he had lost his gorgeous new girlfriend, who was actually his worst enemy, sent in to destroy him. He was in survival mode now and had to focus on fighting the IRS and protecting his assets. Samson considered himself a savvy guy, and he thought he understood pretty well how the world worked. He knew life wasn't fair, so as a general rule, he avoided whining about unfairness. But he was shocked by the crude brutality of what had happened to him.

He recalled the odd comment from Phil S. Stein that he was living in a dream world that would soon be over, and the warning that he wasn't done with him. He made the connection—Phil S. Stein, Delilah, Elliott Mess—and figured it was no coincidence. This wasn't his father's America anymore, the America of the 1950s, of Joe Dimagio, and Gary Cooper, and Marilyn Monroe, and Elvis, and Dinah Shore, and "See the U.S.A. in your Chevrolet." What had happened to him seemed more like the kind of nightmare you would expect in Soviet gulags, or North Korea, or Cuba. But the United States of America? Have we gone that far down the path to tyranny? He wondered how high and how deep this went. Was this just a couple of out-of-control rogue agents who had simply stolen his money? Or was this part of a bigger plan to terrorize ordinary citizens and take us down the final leg of the road to serfdom?

Samson considered his options. He could file a complaint with the local police that he'd been beaten and robbed. But how would it play out? He could tell the police, "I paid off a couple of IRS agents with $200,000 cash that I kept in the basement in a bag, but they got greedy and wanted more so they beat me up." "Uh-huh," he could hear the detective responding. "So you want me to arrest two IRS Special Agents for taking money you owed in taxes?" This obviously wouldn't get him anywhere. Besides, he didn't really want to bring assault charges just because he'd gotten the worst of it; it was against his ethic as a street fighter. He figured a time would come when he could even the score with Elliott Mess with respect to the black eye. And in the meantime, his focus would be on either getting his money back or getting something for his money, i.e a release for all back taxes owed, as had been agreed before Mess stole the receipt.

He decided to contact the IRS directly. But as it turned out, the IRS contacted him first; he found a letter in his mailbox. After reading the disturbing notice, he called the IRS regional office and scheduled an appointment for the next day.

The next day, Samson, who still had a black eye, entered the reception area of the regional office of the IRS, unpleasantly lighted with energy saving fluorescent bulbs. While waiting for his appointment he noticed on the wall an oversized and rather menacing portrait of Darth Vader, dressed all in black of course, except for a purple cape. *What the hell is that about?* he wondered. *Must be a joke.* He was surprised that the IRS apparently had a sense of humor.

His musings about the Darth Vader picture were interrupted by the receptionist calling him in for his appointment with the supervisor. As he entered the supervisor's office, he was surprised by how dimly lit it was. The supervisor sat at his desk with his back to a large window. The contrast of the light at his back, with the lack of light in the room, made it difficult to see his face. All Samson could make out was the silhouette of a man in a trench coat and 1930s-style fedora, seated behind his desk in a large swivel chair. Samson wondered what was wrong with these people, that they all dressed like that. He had the fleeting thought that maybe the IRS had become some kind of cult.

He sat down in front of the desk, as the supervisor took his file from a file cabinet. The supervisor had a lamp on his desk, turned onto Samson, in the style of the old police interrogations. Samson was not intimidated. He turned the lamp around and shined it instead in the supervisor's face. The supervisor was dressed like Elliott Mess but he was older. Samson handed him the notice he'd received in the mail.

"I received this notice," Samson said, putting the paper on the desk. "It says I owe two point four million dollars in back taxes and have to pay two hundred thousand dollars of it immediately."

The supervisor turned the lamp back to shine in Samson's face. "How soon can you pay it?" he asked.

"I already *did* pay it. I gave the agent two hundred thousand dollars as payment in full." As the supervisor looked down at the file, Samson turned the lamp around to shine once again in the supervisor's face.

"We have no record of receiving it. Do you have a canceled check?" The supervisor put the file down, and turned the lamp back toward Samson again, this time holding onto it so Samson couldn't take control of it again.

Samson shielded his eyes from the light, in an exaggerated manner, mocking the crude interrogation tactic. "I paid in cash," he said.

"Do you have a receipt?"

"Yeah, this black eye."

"Huh?"

"No, I don't have a receipt."

"So what do you want?"

Samson noticed that the supervisor had inadvertently loosed his grip on the lamp. So he leaped up and quickly grabbed it. Stretching the chord to its full length, he held it in his lap turned toward the supervisor.

"Well, you could give me my money back."

The supervisor leaned down and unplugged the lamp from the wall. The light went out.

"We don't give money back," he said. Samson placed the darkened lamp on the floor, as the supervisor opened a drawer and picked up a humongous copy of the Internal Revenue Code, thumbing through the pages to find the one he was looking for. "When a taxpayer lacks a receipt or other documentation of payment of taxes," the supervisor continued, "it's covered by section 3602 of the Internal Revenue Code." He perused the page with his finger.

"What does it say?" Samson asked.

"It says you're shit outta luck."

"What? Let me see that!" The supervisor slid the code across the desk to Samson. Samson turned it around, read it, then slammed it shut, and shoved it back across the desk. "It doesn't say that!"

"It's subject to interpretation in the light of catch twenty-three."

"You mean *catch twenty-two?*"

"No, I mean catch twenty-three."

"Catch twenty-three?"

The supervisor stood up, and walked over to the window, looking out, turning his back on Samson. "Catch twenty-three says all government regulations mean whatever we say they mean."

"Can you show me where it says that?"

"No."

"Why not?"

"It's not permitted."

"Not permitted by what?"

"By catch twenty-three."

"Okay, so, in other words, catch twenty-three says it's not permitted for anybody to see catch twenty-three."

"Right."

"So have you seen catch twenty-three?"

"Yes, of course."

"Well so then, if no one is permitted to see it, how come you were permitted to see it?"

"I'm a government official. Government officials are permitted to see it. Ordinary citizens are not permitted to see catch twenty-three."

"Okay, so let me get this straight. Catch twenty-three says that all government regulations mean whatever you say they mean. And catch twenty-three is a government regulation that is subject to catch twenty-three. Therefore if you say that catch twenty-three means that ordinary citizens aren't permitted to see catch twenty-three, then that's what it means because that's what you *say* it means."

"Exactly."

"So where does this catch twenty-three come from?"

"What do you mean where does it come from?"

"I mean—where does it come from?"

"I don't understand that question. That's a meaningless question."

"Okay, how about this. Is it constitutional?"

"Is what constitutional?"

"Catch twenty-three. Is catch twenty-three constitutional?"

"Are you serious? Is that a serious question?"

"Yeah, I'm serious. It's a serious question."

"Look, the Constitution is an historical document."

"Historical document? That's all you think it is?"

"You think it's any more than that anymore?"

"Some of us still believe in it."

"Yeah, some of you still do. You can believe whatever you want."

"Okay, so you don't believe in the Constitution. You think you have the power to make up rules as you go along and that the law means whatever you say it means. You have a picture of Darth Vader in your office. Who the hell are you people?"

"I know you fancy yourself a rugged individualist, Mr. Samson, but you're a dying breed."

"I ain't dead *yet*."

"No, not yet."

"Look, you didn't answer my question," Samson persisted. "Where does this catch twenty-three come from?"

"It doesn't come from anywhere."

"What the hell does that mean?"

"It means it doesn't come from anywhere."

"That's repetitious. You're repeating yourself."

"Your question is absurd. It's an absurd question. It's a non-sequitur."

"How do you figure?"

"It's one of those questions that cannot be answered, that has no answer. Questions like 'Who is John Galt?' or 'Where does God come from?'"

"Look," Samson responded, "I'm not in the habit of discussing metaphysics with government bureaucrats, okay. You're laughing. But you're the one who's being absurd, speaking in riddles. I'm asking you a simple question. This catch twenty-three, is it a statute passed by Congress or what?"

"No, it's not a statute passed by Congress. What is this—twenty questions?"

"If I Google it, what will it say?"

"Nothing, it will say nothing."

"How can it be the law, if there's no information about it, it hasn't been passed by Congress, and it's not authorized by the Constitution?"

The supervisor laughed again. "Catch twenty-three existed before the Constitution, and it still exists after the Constitution. It has always been, and it always will be. And that's just the way it is. And I've told you too much already. I'm not going to say anything else. So unless there's something else, I need to—"

"Yeah, there is something else. Call that agent in here."

"What agent?"

"Elliott Mess."

The supervisor called in Elliott Mess, who came in, and looked down at Samson. "How's your black eye?" he smirked, and sat down.

"How are your balls?" Samson retorted. "Are they black too?"

"Mr. Samson," the supervisor interjected. "That's a violation of Section 9884 of the Internal Revenue Code."

"What is?"

"Making a disparaging comment about an agent's genitals."

"Does that apply to special agents or just regular agents?"

"It applies to *all* agents."

"Uh-huh. And, uh, is this provision of the code also subject to interpretation in the light of catch twenty-three?"

"Of course."

"Well, I didn't actually make a disparaging comment about Agent Mess's genitals," Samson said.

"That's *Special* Agent Mess," Special Agent Mess inserted.

"Right," Samson continued, "I didn't make a disparaging comment about Special Agent Mess's genitals. I was only inquiring about the condition of his balls out of concern after the unfortunate injury he suffered during our conversation the other day. I was reciprocating because Special Agent Mess expressed concern for my eye which was injured during the same conversation."

"You said they were black," the supervisor said.

"Actually I didn't *say* they were black. I've never seen them and I don't know what color they are. I only *asked* if they're black. Not whether they are normally black, as in, from birth, but whether they are black as a result of the blow which they sustained, y'know, like my eye."

"Nevertheless, any intimation that an agent's balls are black, I construe that as a disparaging comment."

"So then, do you also construe it as a disparaging comment to refer to my eye as being black?"

"No, eyes and balls are different."

"Well, do you think there's something wrong with being black?"

"It's not, no, I never—"

"That's racist," Samson accused, figuring that was a good way to go on the offensive.

"Well—" the supervisor stammered, "I, I, uh—"

"Look, I'll tell you what," Samson interrupted. "How about we cut through this racial digression so we can move on to a more pertinent topic? Agent Mess, I mean Special Agent Mess, I withdraw the question and apologize for asking if your balls were black. Okay? And you know what, as a good will gesture, I'll even go a step further. I apologize for letting my face get in the way of your fist as you were swinging it through the air the other day."

There was an awkward silence for a moment as the supervisor and Mess reacted to this unexpected twist. Actually they didn't react. They were indifferent, as reflected in their body language, and complete absence of any facial expression that could be identified with particular emotions. They sat in identical postures with their feet squarely on the ground, their knees apart at a manly distance, wearing indistinguishable fedoras, and similar expressions on their faces. Samson looked back and forth from one to the other repeatedly, as it dawned on him; something wasn't right. "Wait a second," he asked. "Are you guys related?"

Mess and the supervisor, suddenly animated and on guard, as if someone had uncovered a secret they wished to keep hidden, shook their heads and simultaneously said, "No."

The supervisor quickly changed the subject. "Special Agent Mess," he asked, "did you receive two hundred thousand dollars cash from Mr. Samson?"

Samson continued to look back and forth from one to the other incredulously. "You sure you guys aren't related?"

Mess ignored Samson's interruption. "Not that I recall. I'll have to check my records."

"You don't recall? You have to check your records? For two hundred thousand dollars cash?" Samson asked.

"Now, Special Agent Mess, have all your enforcement actions with respect to Mr. Samson been in compliance with the Plan for Universal Compliance?"

"The *what*?" Samson interjected.

"Of course, sir, everything was by the book," Mess replied, still ignoring Samson.

"The Plan for What?" Samson repeated. "Universal Compliance? What the hell is that?"

"Okay, son, good work," the supervisor said.

"You called him son!" exclaimed Samson.

"No, I didn't!" insisted the supervisor, as Mess simultaneously asserted, "No he didn't!"

"Yes, you did! He's your son!" Samson persisted.

"No he's not!" said the supervisor again as Mess said, "No, I'm not!"

"You're his father!"

"No, I'm not!" from the supervisor and "No, he's not!" simultaneously from Mess.

"I'm wasting my time," said Samson. He stood up and stormed out.

As he walked out of the office, through the reception area, he again passed the big picture of Darth Vader. *Maybe it's not a joke*, he thought. As he went out into the parking lot, Samson's mind began working on intellectual constructs to put the bizarre events of recent days into a framework that would make sense of all the weird stuff that was happening to him. He came up with a variety of alternative theories, or maybe more accurately, rough drafts of alternative theories, not as yet thought through in any detail, as to why the world suddenly seemed so strange and hostile. The world had always seemed strange and hostile, but this was a whole new level of strangeness and hostility, better organized and operating from a higher level than the random, ordinary run-of-the-mill strangeness and hostility he'd experienced in the past.

Several possible theories, varying in degrees of plausibility, vaguely flashed through his mind, in those few minutes, most of which seemed to be derived from movies and modern works of fiction. His initial theories included the following:
1. He had fallen down a rabbit hole.
2. The movie *The Matrix* was real. Someone would soon offer him a choice between a red pill and a blue pill.
3. The movie *Star Wars* was real. The dark side of the force was now ascendant throughout the galaxy. Pictures of Darth Vader would soon start showing up everywhere.
4. The U.S. government had been overthrown by a coup d'état, staged by a bunch of whack jobs in fedoras, and the news media hadn't bothered to mention it.

Of these alternative theories, the fourth seemed closest to a plausible reality. Nevertheless Samson recognized that all his notions about the underlying causes of the rapidly deteriorating circumstances of his life were infused with a strain of paranoia. Not that paranoia is necessarily bad. There are times when a healthy dose of paranoia can keep you on your toes, alert to the real dangers that surround us all. Paranoid suspicions aren't exactly alleviated, however, when high level government officials make arbitrary assertions of authority based on mysterious laws like catch twenty-three, which no one had ever heard of but that purportedly, according to said government officials, give them unbounded power to do whatever they damn please, or make passing references to some undefined "Plan for Universal Compliance," a term which, coming from the mouth of an IRS supervisor, had a disturbingly sinister ring to it. It didn't help to discover that the government was sending in sexy female undercover spies on search-and-destroy missions against ordinary citizens.

He wasn't sure about the explanation, but he was certain reality had been altered. Perhaps the veil of illusion had been stripped away, and he was seeing the inner workings of the real world for the first time. He wished he could wake up in his bed and find that this was all just a bad dream. But if he couldn't return to his old familiar universe, then he'd need to figure out how to survive in this alternate one where he had begun to understand that dark mysterious forces were at work behind the scenes exercising power in ways that were not perceptible to the common man. Whether the dark side of the Force was suddenly ascending or whether there was some more prosaic explanation for this bizarre new reality was something he would have to figure out later.

Dubious Philosophical Musings
Tangentially Related to the Story

Part I

Belief

*"The most common of all follies is
to believe passionately in the palpably not true.
It is the chief occupation of mankind."*
—H. L. Mencken

"Courage is the fear of being thought a coward."
—Horace Smith

People believe what they believe because they believe it. We embrace beliefs for a reason; they are useful. They help us simplify reality by organizing the chaos of limitless unconnected bits of information processed by our brains into a coherent understandable whole. The formation of beliefs is necessary for humans to make sense of the universe and function as social beings in an organized society.

But if you ask people to explain the logic of their beliefs, or the thought process by which they arrived at their conclusions, or question their ideas in the manner of Socrates, the intellectual foundation of most beliefs dissolves like a sand castle in the rain. Even if the factual assumptions and logic of their beliefs is exposed to be fallacious, believers are reluctant to abandon or re-examine those beliefs, and they'd rather go through extraordinary mental gymnastics to rationalize clinging to disproven beliefs, rather than make the choice to simply admit they were wrong and change their opinion.

People believe what they believe because that's what they were taught. This is true even among intellectuals who think of themselves as independent thinkers. It's true even for very intelligent people like those reading this book. Although a large portion of the population is capable of understanding ideas, original thought—the independent generation of new ideas—is rare on matters of politics and public policy, culture, religion, and philosophy. Our opinions are largely the product of the ideas to which we've been exposed. That's why the children of Muslims grow up to be Muslims, and the children of Hindus grow up to be Hindus. Children of liberals usually grow up to be liberal, and children of conservatives to be conservative.

There is an exception in cases where the children have extensive exposure to teachers, college professors, religious leaders, or media personalities, who preach a different ideology from the one they learned from their parents. If people convert to a different religion it is usually because someone converted them. If you were a white person raised in the South during segregation you believed in segregation. If you were born in a communist country you believed in communism.

Most people only abandon the ideologies they are taught if somewhere along the way, someone subverted those ideologies and taught them new ones. If a 10-year-old boy is indoctrinated with the notion that Allah wants him to murder infidels and will reward him in heaven for such carnage with 72 virgins, then that is what he'll believe. And to him this is "God's truth," even though to anyone else in the world with half a brain it is patent nonsense.

It's astonishing that, based on the creativity and insights of a tiny fraction of the population, the human species has had extraordinary achievements in the fields of science, technology, medicine, philosophy, law, and the arts. These achievements have occurred despite the fact that humans tend to believe whatever we are taught, as a result of which we are prone to embrace ideologies which embody mind-numbing stupidity and ignorance on a massive scale. It is this intellectual gullibility that makes us vulnerable to oppression and enslavement.

Chapter 10
Paradise Lost

"My entire life the government has been my enemy. When it has not been trying to silence me it has been trying to rob me. I have never had any contact with it that was not an attack on my security and an affront to my dignity."
—H. L. Mencken

"Look out kid. It's somethin' you did. God knows when, but you're doin' it again. They must bust in early May. Orders from the DA."
—Bob Dylan

Samson knew he was up against a big adversary, even bigger than Pete. And he knew he didn't yet grasp the dimensions of the situation. He decided to try to carry on with his normal life to see how this would play out, while at the same time preparing for the worst. On his way to the car lot he stopped at the bank to make a cash withdrawal. But the teller told him his account lacked sufficient funds.

"There must be a mistake," he insisted. "I've got twenty-five thousand dollars in that account."

The teller pushed some keys on the computer. "According to this, you have a balance of zero."

Samson understood what the sudden disappearance of the funds in his bank account signified and had a good idea where this was heading. If he was going to make a run for it, he'd need to raise cash and he needed to do it fast. He figured his best chance was to get to his car lot, where he had some cash in a safe. He could raise some more by selling some cars as quickly as possible. He drove up to the front gate, but he was too late; the lot was locked shut with a huge padlock. All the cars were gone. There were no customers or employees. The "Repossessed Cars for Sale" sign was being taken down by workmen. Samson saw a sign on the front of the building: "PROPERTY OF U.S. GOVERNMENT—Keep Out." He drove off.

Samson had to think fast. It was obvious the government was going to take everything he had. But he didn't know whether they were also going to arrest him. He still had more than $10,000 in cash at home that he hadn't given to Elliott Mess. He also had a passport. *If worse comes to worst*, he thought, *I can get the hell out of the country*. He was starting to feel like he didn't want to live in a country where such things could happen anyway. He could always move somewhere where he might have more freedom, like, say, Cuba. Okay, bad example. How about Switzerland, or Singapore, or the Cayman Islands?

Samson slowly drove up the street to his house. He didn't see any government agents around so he pulled into the driveway. He was unaware that an IRS drone had been tracking him since he left his car lot. Elliott Mess quickly drove around the corner and pulled in behind Samson, blocking his car. Samson turned off his engine and got out of the car. There was no point trying to flee on foot. He was thinking about how he could get into the house to get the cash and passport before Mess figured out what he was doing. A tow truck that had been passing by suddenly turned into his driveway. At the same time a large moving van was just pulling up to park in the street in front of his house. To his surprise, Samson found himself admiring, with some detachment, the government's impressive efficiency in carrying out this operation. *Amazing,* he thought, *that the government is so bad at everything else, and so good at fucking people over.*

Mess and another agent got out of the car. Mess signaled to the tow truck driver, who pulled into the driveway, and began hooking up to the back of Samson's car. Three men got out of the moving van and walked toward Samson's house. Samson thought the other agent with Mess looked familiar, but he was having trouble placing him. Then he realized it was the drug dealer, who had tried to entrap him, but now he was dressed like an IRS agent. He smirked at Samson. Samson smirked back and said, "I didn't recognize you without your earring."

Mess handed Samson an official document. "Mr. Sam Samson, we have orders to seize your cars, airplane, all personal possessions, stocks, bonds, your business assets, rental properties, bank accounts, and your home."

"I'll pack my stuff," Samson said.

"Don't bother. We get all your stuff." Mess pointed to the moving van, which was now backing into the driveway.

"Is that all?" Samson asked.

"Yeah, that's all."

Samson turned momentarily toward his car, but the tow truck had already hooked up to it. He started to walk away down the street.

"Oh, yeah, there is one other thing," Mess remembered. Samson stopped in his tracks. "You're also under arrest."

The drug dealer agent and Mess grabbed Samson from behind, pulled his hands behind his back, and handcuffed him. The drug dealer agent bent down, forced Samson's legs apart, and patted him down. While Mess stood behind Samson holding one arm, the drug dealer agent came around in front of him.

"You don't look like such a hot shot now, do you?" he gloated. "You are charged with failing to file tax returns, evading federal income taxes, and assaulting an officer of the U.S. Treasury Department. You have a right to remain silent. Anything you say can and will be used against you in a court of law. You have a right to an attorney. If you can't afford an attorney, which you can't because we took all your money, then one will be appointed by the court." Then softly in Samson's ear he added, "But it won't do you any good anyway, pal, because we're gonna nail your ass to the wall."

"Hey, I gotta question," Samson said.

"What?" Mess said.

"You got any gum?"

Chapter 11
Catch 23

"The American Republic will endure until the day Congress discovers that it can bribe the public with the public's money."
—Alexis de Tocqueville

*"How does it feel? To be on your own, With no direction home,
A complete unknown
Just like a rolling stone."*
—Bob Dylan

Isaac was there when the federal agents swarmed into Spoilsport Motors. Isaac wasn't just Samson's top salesman and right-hand man; he was also his best friend. Isaac was charming, especially with women, and had worked for Samson for six years. Some day he planned to start his own car lot, and figured when the time came, Samson would reward him for his loyalty by helping him get started. Isaac knew what to do when the federal agents showed up. Before they had a chance to take control of the place, he removed the contents of the safe, about $8,000 cash, and hid it in his shoes. Together with some of his own money, and money he borrowed from relatives, he raised enough to bail Samson out.

The first thing Samson did when he got out of jail was to go see his congressman, Les Moore. As Samson entered his office,

Congressman Moore, a portly middle-aged man, was saluting the flag by himself. Samson stood behind him, unnoticed, waiting for him to finish. Congressman Moore finished saluting and noticed Samson behind him. "Are you Sam Samson?" he asked. Samson nodded. "Would you like to join me in a verse of 'God Bless America' before we begin?"

"Uh, no thanks, I'm a little hoarse from singing 'The Star Spangled Banner' on the way over here," Samson answered.

They sat down and Congressman Moore began, "I know why you're here, Mr. Samson. You wanna know if I can help get the IRS off your back."

"Can you?"

"No."

Samson stood up to leave.

"Now understand, Mr. Samson. I'm very proud of my record of constituent service. When the voters in my district have bureaucratic problems with government agencies no one is better than Les Moore about getting…"

"Bureaucratic problems?" Samson interrupted. "This is no bureaucratic problem. Those S.O.Bs have destroyed—"

"That's exactly the point," Congressman Moore interrupted. "You're not talking about a little bit of red tape here that can be fixed with a phone call, y'know. This is—"

"Okay, I get it. There's something big going on here. I don't understand it, and maybe you don't even understand it. Does it have something to do with this 'Plan for Universal Compliance' or whatever the hell it is?"

"Plan for Universal Compliance? You know about that?"

"Yeah, the IRS supervisor let it slip. What the hell is it?"

"I don't know," said Congressman Moore, suddenly speaking in a hushed tone and looking around as if to see if anybody else was listening, which struck Samson as a tad silly, as they were the only two people in the office. "There have been rumors, but I didn't know it had gone into effect already. What did he say about it?"

"He asked the IRS agent if he had followed it. That was it. So what is it? The Plan for Universal Compliance?"

"It's not something that should be talked about. There are security issues. I don't know the specifics. I don't think you should mention this to anyone. It's not safe. I can say no more."

"Say no more. How about catch twenty-three. Can you say anything about that?"

"My God. You know about that too? How did you learn all this? Never mind. I can say no more."

"Say no more."

"Your life could be in danger. I can say no more. Sorry I can't help you."

"I came in here because I thought it's your job…"

"It's my job to get elected."

"Well, maybe I could help you get elected."

"Can you make a campaign contribution?"

"No, they took all my money."

"Frankly, Mr. Samson, you're useless to me. And besides, when the IRS doesn't like somebody, I stay out of their way."

"You're scared of the IRS?"

"I'm not scared; I *love* the IRS."

"You love the IRS."

"Yeah, why shouldn't I? They work for *me*."

"The IRS works for *you*."

"Well, after a fashion. Look, Mr. Samson, politics is a business. It's big business. I'm in the giving away money business.

And the IRS supplies the money. So I scratch their backs; they scratch mine. Get it? But I'll tell you what. I'm planning to run for the Senate. If you can come up with a hundred and fifty thousand cash I could help. I can't get you your assets back, but I might be able to keep you out of jail."

"It's no use," Samson replied. "They took all my money."

Before he left, Samson asked whether anyone had ever had the courage to stand up to the IRS.

"Oh, yeah," Congressman Moore said, "there was one fellow, Congressman George Hansen. He took them on big time. The guy had a lotta guts."

"Well, maybe I should go see this Congressman Hansen," Samson said. "Maybe he could help."

"Y'know, that's a great idea. You could learn a lot from Congressman Hansen. I'll give you his address. You go talk to him and let me know how it goes." Congressman Moore wrote the address on a Post-it and handed it to Samson.

...

The next day, Samson went to pay a visit to Congressman Hansen. But the only building at the address Congressman Moore had given him was a federal prison. Samson paced up and down the street looking for the nonexistent office building, thinking he must have been given a mistaken address. Then he realized there was no mistake. He entered the prison and inquired at the front desk if a Congressman George Hansen was there. And he was – as an inmate.

Samson was unable to get in to see Congressman Hansen. So he went to the library and did an online search. He learned that George Hansen was a seven-term congressman from Idaho who conducted hearings into IRS abuses of power and wrote a book entitled, *To Harass Our People,* which documented unconstitutional practices and chronic abuse of power by the IRS. (Author note: Google it!) The government retaliated against Hansen by prosecuting and convicting him, purportedly for failing to make full disclosure of his wife's assets on his congressional financial disclosure form.

This offense is usually considered a minor infraction, not worthy of criminal prosecution. But an exception was made for this renegade congressman who had dared to go up against the IRS, and the full power of the U.S. Attorney General's office was brought to bear to convict him. As it turns out, Congresswoman Geraldine Ferraro, who was the Democratic nominee for vice president in 1984, was guilty of the same failure to disclose her spouse's assets, but was not prosecuted. George Hansen was a political prisoner. Samson understood the message: Don't fight the IRS. Unfortunately, it was too late.

Chapter 12
Anthem

"There's something happening here. What it is ain't exactly clear.... There's a man with a gun over there, telling me that I got to beware."
—Buffalo Springfield

"I believe there is something out there watching us. Unfortunately, it's the government."
—Woody Allen

Having lost his home, Sam was staying in Isaac's apartment. The first night he slept on the sofa bed, tossing and turning. He had a dream that he was in the famous 1984 Apple Computer Super Bowl commercial. (Author note: The 1984 commercial was a totalitarian nightmare, drawing on George Orwell's famous book, *1984*. The commercial featured a room with hundreds of mesmerized zombie-like men sitting in rows, staring vacantly at a huge telescreen of Big Brother, who brainwashed them with a torrent of propaganda. A beautiful woman dressed like an ancient Olympic athlete ran gracefully into the room in slow motion, carrying a big sledge-hammer, and defiantly flung it through the telescreen.) In Samson's dream he was in the role played by the female runner, carrying the sledge hammer. Big Brother, on the huge screen, in the deep voice of the IRS commissioner, boomed surrealistically as if in an echo chamber: "All dissenters have been brought into conformity. The enemies of the state have been destroyed. We have attained universal compliance with the code, universal compliance with the code, universal compliance with the code."

Samson ran fearlessly into the room with the sledgehammer, running past rows of brainwashed people, but before he could throw it through the telescreen, Delilah came up in front of him, distracting him from his mission. She embraced him and kissed him. He kissed her and held her tight, but she pulled away. She looked behind her and seeing Elliott Mess, ran over and threw her arms around him. Like Judas, she pointed Samson out to Mess. Samson pulled his attention away from Delilah and started back toward the huge screen, raising the sledge hammer, and ready to throw it. But before he could act, Mess and several uniformed men with guns surrounded him. They grabbed him and took the sledgehammer. Samson looked over at Delilah, but she averted her gaze, as he was helplessly carried outside and placed in front of a firing squad.

The pregnant lady who he'd helped at the car lot appeared, dressed all in white, no longer pregnant and carrying her new baby in her arms. She rushed to stand between him and the firing squad, but was whisked off by guards, screaming. As the firing squad took aim, Samson saw Delilah passionately kissing Elliott Mess. He cried out "Delilah" as the firing squad opened fire on him. The dream ended. Samson woke up in a sweat, the name of his betrayer, "Delilah" still on his lips.

Dawn was breaking as Samson got out of bed. He brushed his teeth, showered, and sat down on the couch for his morning

Transcendental Meditation. He closed his eyes and went deep inside himself, into the silence, dissolving the nocturnal gloom and foreboding he had felt on waking from the disturbing dream. When he came out of meditation, he felt his strength renewed; he was ready for the battle.

Chapter 13
The Trial

"The makers of the Constitution conferred, as against the government, the right to be left alone—the most comprehensive of rights and the right most valued by civilized men."
—Justice Louis Brandeis

"The prince should always be generous with other people's money, but never with his own."
—Machiavelli

Samson knew he couldn't win the case based on the facts or the law. He had no proof that IRS agents had stolen his money and assaulted him, and figured the jury would never believe his story. His best hope was to appeal to the jury's sense of justice, to persuade them that the whole system is oppressive. So he went to the library and began his research, taking out books on the Constitution, the Founding Fathers, freedom, and the history of the income tax.

At his arraignment he was heartened to see that the prosecuting attorney was Phil S. Stein. Samson thought Stein was a fool, and he was surprised Stein was smart enough to have gotten through law school. He thought of Stein as a bureaucrat, a category of people for whom Samson had contempt, and was thankful the government hadn't found somebody smarter to prosecute his case. Unfortunately for Samson, he underestimated Stein. Stein was obnoxious, but he wasn't stupid.

The judge, the honorable Shirley Eujest, gaveled the proceedings to order. "Where's your attorney, Mr. Samson?" she asked.

"I can't afford an attorney, your honor. Elliott Mess took my money."

"Well, that's not surprising; he's an IRS agent."

"Special agent," Elliott Mess interjected from the back of the courtroom. Samson turned around, surprised by the sound of Mess's voice. He hadn't expected him to be there.

"Yes, well, 'special agent.' In any event, if you're indigent, Mr. Samson, the court can appoint an attorney."

"I'm not indigent; I'm American," Samson said.

"Indigent just means without means, y'know, poor," said the judge.

"I know that; I'm not ignorant. And I'm not poor. I'm just broke."

"I'm not going to split hairs with you over semantics, sir. You have a right to an attorney—"

"Yeah, I've heard that."

"Mr. Samson, this is a court of law, and I am the judge. I have no tolerance for being interrupted by defendants. Is that understood?"

"Yes, your honor."

"If you can't afford an attorney, then the court will appoint one."

"Well, if I can't afford an attorney, and you appoint one, who will pay him?"

"The government."

"No thanks, your honor. I'd rather represent myself."

"Well, you have serious federal charges against you, and you need assistance from competent counsel."

"Your honor, as you've pointed out, I have a right to an attorney. I believe I also have a right to *not* have an attorney...." And so it went. After a good bit of back and forth, the judge reluctantly agreed to let him represent himself.

Samson's trial began three months later. Phil S. Stein had Elliott Mess and the other agent who visited him that first day testify about their encounter with Samson, modifying certain details. They included an account of Samson's assault on Mess, omitting, of course, any mention of the $200,000 cash Samson had given Mess, the receipt, or that Mess had struck the first blow. Samson didn't bother to cross examine them. Then Stein called Delilah, who validated the car lot computer accounting records and other incriminating evidence.

On cross examination, Samson asked her whether working as an IRS undercover agent was a full-time job. She said it was, more or less. He asked whether the government regulations for undercover agents have any guidelines about romantic liaisons with the targets of investigations.

"That's not encouraged," she conceded.

"Do you always throw in the fringe benefits?" Samson asked.

"Objection!" Stein interjected, leaping to his feet.

"Sustained," said the judge. "That's too vague. No one knows for sure what you mean by 'fringe benefits.'"

"Of course they do," Samson said. "Everyone knows what fringe benefits are. But I'll be more explicit. How about this? Do you always have sex with the people you're investigating?"

There was a stir in the courtroom.

"No," she answered quietly.

"What was that? I didn't hear you."

"No," she repeated.

"But you had sex with me, didn't you?"

Delilah didn't answer.

"Could you answer the question please?

"Yes."

"Yes, what?"

"Yes, I had sex with you."

"It was pretty good, wasn't it?" Samson asked.

"Objection!" Stein said. "Irrelevant."

"That's okay," Samson said. "I withdraw the question. No further questions."

In a surprise move, Stein called Sam Samson. Samson stood up to walk to the stand, but the judge stopped him. "You have a right, Mr. Samson," she said, "against self-incrimination, under the fifth amendment. You don't have to testify."

"That's very kind of you," Samson replied, "but I better get up there and defend myself, or else these good folks on the jury might believe the bad things the persecuting attorney says about me."

After Samson was sworn in, Stein approached the bench and handed the judge some documents. "Your honor," he said. "I introduce as Peoples' Exhibit 'D', IRS records showing the defendant has only filed a tax return once since 1994. And on that return he falsely reported only fourteen thousand dollars in income."

"Your honor, I object to this evidence," Samson interjected.

The judge looked over the top of her bifocals down her nose at Samson. "On what grounds?"

"On the grounds that it might incriminate me."

"That's what we're here for, Mr. Samson. Objection overruled."

Stein moved over to stand in front of the witness stand. "Mr. Samson, would you please tell the jury why you didn't file any tax returns from 1994 to 2011?"

"I forgot."

"That's it?" Stein asked.

"Yeah."

"That's your defense?"

"Yeah."

"You forgot?"

"Yeah, I already told you three times. You got a problem with that?"

Stein looked at the jury to convey his incredulity at this flimsy answer. "Yeah, I do," he said. "You couldn't have forgotten every year for seventeen years. Why didn't you file?"

"It was an oversight."

"An oversight."

"Yeah."

"For seventeen years."

"Yeah, well, uh, see that was Tom Daschle's explanation and it worked pretty well for him."

"Tom Daschle?"

"Yeah, you know, Senator Tom Daschle, the former Senate Majority Leader."

"I know who Tom Daschle is," Stein said.

"Yeah well, Tom Daschle cheated the IRS out of one hundred forty thousand dollars. And he told Congress it was an oversight. So, you see, mine was an oversight too."

"Move to strike, your honor."

"Sustained," said the judge. "The jury will disregard Mr. Samson's comments about Tom Daschle."

"Mr. Samson," Stein continued. "Can we get a straight answer why you didn't file tax returns for seventeen years?"

"I didn't want to."

"You didn't want to."

"No."

"Why not?"

"'Cause I'm a musician. And musicians believe money is to spend."

"Yeah?"

"Yeah."

"A musician, huh. What instrument do you play?"

"Triangle."

Stein stepped back to the prosecutor's table officiously and picked up a document.

Your honor, I'd like to introduce as Peoples' exhibit E a list of items seized from Mr. Samson's home. Stein gave a copy to the judge, then walked to the witness stand and handed exhibit E to Samson. "Would you please identify this document?" he asked.

"Yeah, that's a list of all my stuff the IRS took when they stole my house."

"Motion to strike, Your honor, the comment about stealing his house."

"Granted. The jury will disregard Mr. Samson's comment about the IRS stealing his house."

"But the IRS *did* steal my house!" Samson interjected.

"Mr. Samson," the judge said. "When I've ruled, I've ruled. You understand that?"

"Sure."

"Now, Mr. Samson," Stein continued. "Do you see a 'triangle' shown on this list?"

Samson handed the list back without looking at it. "No."

"So there was no triangle in your home at the time of your arrest."

"Nope."

"Yet you claim to be a triangle player."

"Yeah."

Stein, thinking he'd scored points with this clever ploy, looked over at the jury triumphantly, but the jurors didn't look that impressed. "Well, looks like we caught you in a little inconsistency here," he said, looking back at Samson.

"No you didn't."

"How do you explain the discrepancy?"

"I rent."

"You rent."

"Yeah."

"You rent what?"

"A triangle. From a music store."

"I don't understand."

"When I need a triangle, I rent one from a music store."

"Well, when was the last time you rented a triangle?"

"Don't remember."

Stein noticed that a couple of jurors were rolling their eyes, but he wasn't sure whether it was because they thought Samson was ridiculous or whether they might think *he* was ridiculous. It occurred to him that Samson had lured him into a silly digression and he wanted to get back on track. "Uh huh," he said. "So you've got some pretty compelling reasons for not paying your taxes: you forgot, it was an oversight, you don't want to - and you're a musician. Is that it?

"Well, there's one other thing." Samson hesitated, reluctant to give what might sound like another lame excuse. "See, economists say that tax cuts stimulate the economy..."

"Yeah, and so what's the point?"

"So I gave myself a tax cut."

"A tax cut."

"Yeah, I felt it was my patriotic duty to help stimulate the American economy, with a tax cut."

"Patriotic duty?"

"Yeah."

"To cheat on taxes."

"Yeah. I'm willing to make my share of sacrifice to help my country."

"Sacrifice, huh."

Samson shrugged his shoulders.

"And what about filling out false tax returns?" Stein continued. "You think that's your patriotic duty too?"

"Sure."

"You think it's okay to lie?"

"Yeah. It depends on the circumstances. I mean if someone's trying to rob you..."

"Yeah, but nobody was trying to rob you," Stein interrupted.

"No? What do *you* call it?"

"What?"

"When the IRS takes all your money."

"That's not robbery; it's *taxes*."

"Look, if a man with a gun comes to your door and says you have to give him all your money. Isn't that robbery? Does the fact that he has a badge mean that it isn't robbery?"

"No, if he has a badge, it means it's taxes."

"And if you refuse he'll seize your home and everything you've got, and put you in jail. That doesn't sound like robbery to you?"

"Sounds pretty farfetched."

"Farfetched? That's what happened to *me*!"

"No, Mr. Samson, in America our tax system is based on voluntary compliance."

"Voluntary compliance, huh? Then I guess I'll just leave now." Samson started to stand up. The judge pounded her gavel. A guard in the back of the courtroom cocked his pistol and took aim at Samson as he called for backup. Samson froze, halfway out of his seat. A second guard ran into the courtroom, his pistol drawn also. Samson slowly sat back down. The guards holstered their pistols. Samson turned to the jury. "Voluntary compliance," he said.

The jury and spectators laughed nervously at these theatrics. The judge, irritated, turned to Samson imperiously. "Mr. Samson, you don't seem to be taking these proceedings very seriously. Are you trying to show contempt for this court?"

"No, I'm trying to conceal it."

The judge pounded her gavel again. "That's it. I'm going to fine you a thousand dollars."

"For contempt of court?"

"Plagiarism."

"Plagiarism?" Samson asked incredulously.

"Yeah, you took that line from Mae West."

"But, your honor, try to be fair."

"I *am* trying."

"Yeah you're *very* trying."

"Another thousand dollars."

"Contempt of court?"

"No, plagiarism again. You took that line from Groucho Marx."

"Oy vey."

"Another thousand dollars."

"Plagiarism?"

"Contempt of court."

"Fine. Fine me all you want." Samson looked at Elliott Mess. "Elliott, take three thousand from the two hundred thousand you stole from me and give it to the judge." Samson felt events had become so bizarre that he had nothing to lose. "You know, at this point," he added, "I don't really care what you do because I know you're all nothing but a pack of cards."

"Mr. Samson," the judge shot back. "If you think we're a pack of cards, perhaps you would have grounds to change your plea to 'not guilty by reason of insanity.' If you decide to do that please file a motion after lunch, and the court will order a psychiatric evaluation. In the meantime, I've had about all I can take of your sense of humor for one morning, so the court will recess until one-thirty." She pounded her gavel.

"Actually, your honor," Samson said as everyone got up and started leaving the courtroom, "you can complain about my humor, but off the record, you were doing a pretty good job as straight man, y'know, with the jokes about plagiarism and contempt of court." It wouldn't hurt, Samson was thinking, to try a little repartee with the judge, to maybe establish a better rapport.

"What jokes?" she asked coldly as she stood up, turned her back to him, and headed out of the room.

Chapter 14

And God Created Woman

"A woman never forgives a man for the wrong she does him."
    —Somerset Maugham

"Ain't it hard when you discover that—he really wasn't where it's at. After he took from you everything he could steal."
    —Bob Dylan

Samson stood up on the witness stand and ran after Delilah, who was heading out the door. He caught up with her from behind as she walked out of the courtroom.

She was walking quickly, slightly ahead of Samson, as she went out of the courthouse and headed across the street to the sheltered parking lot. It was a windy day, but not too cold, and she was wearing a light overcoat, which was open. Samson couldn't help thinking how good she looked and what great legs she had, although that was the last thing he wanted to be thinking about. She remained ahead of him as they entered the parking lot, obviously not eager to be engaged in conversation.

"Why do you do this?" he asked.

"It's what I do. Why do you sell cars?"

"How much do you get?"

"Ten percent. Plus living expenses."

Samson grabbed Delilah's wrist from behind her, stopping her from moving forward, and pulled her around forcing her to face him.

"You flush my life down the toilet for ten percent?"

She yanked her wrist free from his grip and hit him in the chest with both hands, with an intensity of force that surprised him, shoving him backwards. "Plus living expenses," she said. "Besides it's your own stupid fault. You shouldn't have hit Elliott in the balls. That makes him mad."

"Why? Is that something that happens to him often?"

"More often than you might think." She started walking quickly again and reached her car, with Samson close behind. She opened the car door and got in.

Samson held her car door open so she couldn't shut it, while leaning against the roof of the car with his other hand. "Y'know, you're right," he said. "Next time some thug steals two hundred thousand dollars from me and punches me in the face, I'll try being nicer to him!"

"You know what your problem is?" she shot back. "You lack diplomatic skills. Don't you know you catch more flies with honey than vinegar?"

"I'm not trying to catch flies. I'm trying to get rid of assholes."

"Well, maybe you can get rid of more assholes with honey."

"I don't think so. These assholes don't care about honey."

She pulled hard on the car door, and he moved aside, letting her close it. But to his surprise, she lowered her window. "Why did you pay him in cash?"

"We made a deal. I didn't know he was a crook. I used to watch him on TV."

"TV?"

"Y'know. 'The Untouchables.'"

"That wasn't him." She shook her head in disbelief.

He leaned over and put his hands on the ledge of the car window. "So tell me the truth. Were the fringe benefits just part of the job?"

Softening, she put her hand over his hand. "No, babe. That was just 'cause you're cute. And I don't regret it; it was great."

"You're a real Jezebel, Delilah."

"You don't understand, Sam. How was I supposed to know?"

"How were you supposed to know what?"

"Y'know. That I was gonna fall for you. By then it was too late."

"So what are you saying? That you didn't fuck me until after you'd already fucked me?"

"No, actually, I think it was just the opposite."

"Ah, so you fucked me *before* you fucked me."

"No, it was the other way around. Well, actually your terminology is a little confusing. I'm not sure which time you're using the word in the literal sense and which time in the figurative. I turned in all your financial records to the IRS *before* we had sex. Does that answer your question? But I'll make it up to you, Sam. I'll visit you in prison."

"I'm not going to prison."

"It's no use, Sam. You *are* going to prison."

"Not if I'm acquitted."

"You're not gonna be acquitted."

"How do you know?"

"Didn't you know? The fix is in. But don't worry. I'll be waiting for you when you get out."

"Good to know you're on my side, Delilah," he said with exaggerated sarcasm. Against his better judgment, under the influence no doubt of the estrogen effect, he kissed her. It was intended as a small, brief kiss, but she didn't let go. She kissed him back with a level of passion that caught him off guard, that reminded him how fabulous she was, and conveyed to him, leaving no room for doubt, that he was more to her than just another work assignment. She held onto him like she didn't want to let go. *Is it possible?* he wondered. He turned and walked away, as she started her car and drove off.

Chapter 15
Jezebel

*"It went on yesterday and it's going on tonight.
Somewhere there's somebody ain't treating somebody right.
All through the shadows, watch 'em come and watch 'em go.
Only one thing in common. They got the fire down below."*
—Bob Seger

*"Everybody knows that the dice are loaded.
Everybody rolls with their fingers crossed.
Everybody knows that the war is over.
Everybody knows the good guys lost.
Everybody knows the fight was fixed.
The poor stay poor, the rich get rich.
Thats how it goes. Everybody knows."*
—Leonard Cohen

Delilah wasn't known for having a highly developed moral compass, and in any event, she was an IRS agent, albeit an unusually sexy one. But she never let her emotions interfere with her work. If she was in love with Samson, no one would know it. She arranged a private meeting with Buddha, who, as Samson's bookkeeper, could be a helpful witness for the prosecution. They sat across from each other at a booth at the Cadillac Cafe, drinking coffee, speaking furtively.

"They want you to testify against him," she said.

"You work for *them*?" Buddha asked.

"You didn't know?"

"Forget it. I want nothing to do with this."

"They'll pay you."

"They can't pay me enough."

"Why? What's the problem?"

"You don't understand. Samson was the only one who would hire me when I got out of prison."

Delilah leaned forward across the table, speaking softly. "Look, Buddha. I like Samson. I like him a lot. But there's nothing you can do. If you don't play ball you'll be implicated as an accomplice and they'll revoke your parole. Samson is going to prison anyway. What are you gonna gain by going with him?"

"Does the word 'loyalty' have any meaning for you?"

"Well, I—"

"Look," Buddha interrupted. "There's gotta be a way outta this."

Chapter 16
The Loan Ranger

"A government that robs Peter to pay Paul can always depend upon the support of Paul."
—George Bernard Shaw

"Giving money and power to government is like giving whiskey and car keys to teenage boys."
—P. J. O'Rourke

The trial resumed that afternoon with Samson still on the witness stand.

"Mr. Samson," Stein began. "How would our government function if people didn't pay taxes?" Stein thought he was going for the jugular with this question, but it was, in fact, an extremely stupid tactic. He should have stayed singularly focused on the question whether Samson paid his taxes. Instead he was moving the discussion right on to Samson's turf.

"The same way it functioned for a hundred and twenty-five years, before we had an income tax," Samson answered.

"Taxes are the price we pay for civilization, Mr. Samson."

"Then we're getting more 'civilization' than we need. Do you have any idea how much money the federal government wastes? They give away twenty-four billion dollars a year to corrupt foreign governments; fifty-two billion to put people who don't like to work in crime-infested slum units; ninety-five billion to pay millionaire farmers not to grow food; two hundred billion to defend Europe and Japan. And who are they defending them from anyway? A trillion dollars to fight a useless war in Afghanistan.

"They spend seven hundred and twenty-eight billion for health care, which is enough to make you sick. Twenty three billion for the energy department so we can achieve energy independence. That's worked pretty well, huh? Five hundred thousand to restore Lawrence Welk's house, three hundred thousand to remodel the congressional beauty parlor, one point nine million for the Pleasure Beach Water Taxi Service project, and one point eight million for swine odor and manure management. They spent sixty billion dollars bailing out failed auto makers, one hundred and seventy-five billion to bail out the failed AIG insurance company, and eight hundred and fifty billion dollars to bail out a bunch of failed banks.

"They spent four hundred and twenty thousand to study the correct use of condoms. That must be for the benefit of people like Mr. Stein; the rest of us figured out how to use condoms in high school. The IRS alone spent fifty million dollars on a bunch of extravagant and totally useless employee conferences, where they made parody 'Star Trek' videos that cost sixty thousand dollars. That's a good use of taxpayer money, huh?

"The government goes through three point eight trillion dollars a year, has run up seventeen trillion dollars in debt, which they can't pay back! And people like me, and the jurors, have to pay for all this waste, useless bureaucracy, corruption, and fraud. That's your idea of civilization, Mr. Phil S. Stein?"

Up to this point, Stein, who was now seated casually on counsel's table, had felt the trial was going his way. *But this could be a turning point*, he thought, as it dawned on him that he'd made a mistake by opening this can of worms. But he couldn't just leave it hanging out there. He knew Samson's argument was resonating with the jury, as jurors were looking at Samson thoughtfully, and some of them had even been nodding their heads in agreement as he spoke. "So you feel that because the government wastes money, you shouldn't have to pay taxes?" he rejoined.

"Yeah."

"But what if everybody felt the way you do?"

"Then I'd be a damn fool to feel any other way."

The judge looked down sternly at Samson. "A thousand dollars. Joseph Heller."

Stein stood back up, consciously seeking to show the jury with his body language that he wasn't defeated by Samson's argument, and he was ready to go back on the offensive. He walked back toward the witness stand. "Aren't you being selfish, Mr. Samson?" he asked. "Of course the government's not perfect. But the people of America depend on government. The poor need welfare. Retirees need Social Security. Businesses depend on subsidies. Farmers, on price supports. Students need loans, and home buyers need mortgages. Everybody wants something from Uncle Sam."

"Yeah, exactly. Everybody's looking for a handout."

"Uh-huh. Everybody's looking for a handout, except you, right? You don't want anything from the government, do you, Mr. Samson?"

"I wanna be left alone."

"You don't want Social Security when you get old?"

"No."

"You don't want highways?"

"If it means having Elliott Mess at my door, I'd rather ride a horse."

Although this sounded like a flip answer, the truth is Samson meant it. He'd often felt that he was born in the wrong century, that he would gladly have suffered the hardships of life before the invention of modern conveniences like electricity, plumbing, and internal combustion engines, in exchange for the freedom of life in the Wild West. He would have been happier in that world where he could have ridden free on the range without traffic cops and traffic lights, photo radar and speeding tickets, DMV officials and IRS agents, licensing boards, zoning boards, planning commissions, truth in lending laws, blue sky laws, safety and environmental regulations, insider trading rules, and Social Security numbers. And without having to put up with the likes of Elliott Mess and Phil S. Stein. He even closed his eyes for a moment and indulged in a little daydream, which briefly took him out of the courtroom and back into those "exciting days of yesteryear."

He imagined himself and a woman on horses galloping next to each other at high speed through the prairie in the Old West. Two men on horseback hid behind a rock on a hillside watching them. The two men swooped down at a gallop chasing after them. It looked like the Lone Ranger and Tonto chasing outlaws as they did in so many old tv episodes. But as it turned out, it was actually Phil S. Stein, dressed in a Lone Ranger outfit complete with mask, only he was also wearing a sheriff's badge. The man with him was Pete, impersonating the Lone Ranger's faithful Indian companion, Tonto. Sheriff Stein and Tonto/Pete caught up with Samson and his companion, Delilah, both of them wearing old west clothes, Delilah attired like Dale Evans. Sheriff Stein motioned for Samson and Delilah to pull over and stop, which they did, still mounted.

"What seems to be the problem, sheriff?" Samson asked.

"May I see your driver's license and vehicle registration?" Sheriff Stein said, more of a command than a question.

Samson and Delilah stared at him blankly as if they didn't know what he was talking about. But the sheriff waited them out. They reluctantly took out their wallets, removed their licenses, and handed them to the sheriff.

"I don't know what happened to the registration," said Samson. "I put it in the horse's glove compartment, but I guess it blew off."

Sheriff Stein looked at Samson's driver's license. "Well, Mr. Samson. I clocked you going fifteen miles per hour in a ten-mile-per-hour zone. You also changed lanes back there without using a turn signal."

"Horses don't have turn signals," Delilah observed.

"Do you have proof of insurance?" Sheriff Stein asked.

"What?" Samson asked.

"Proof of insurance. State law requires all vehicles to carry liability insurance."

"This isn't a vehicle; it's a horse."

"Why do you need insurance?" Delilah asked.

"In case there's a collision," Sheriff Stein explained.

"A collision between horses?" Samson asked.

"I don't make the laws, Mr. Samson; I just enforce them."

Tonto/Pete leaned over to Sheriff Stein and gestured toward Samson and Delilah.

"Them not wearing seatbelts, Kemo Sabe," he said

"Will you excuse us a moment?" Sheriff Stein said to Samson and Delilah. He turned his back on them and took Pete/Tonto aside several feet away, still mounted on the horses, their backs toward Samson and Delilah. He leaned over toward Pete/Tonto and whispered, "I've told you a hundred times, Tonto! Don't call me 'Kemo Sabe' in *front* of people! It's embarrassing."

Sheriff Stein and Tonto moved back toward Samson and Delilah. The sheriff wrote up two tickets and handed one to each of them. "I've cited you for exceeding the speed limit, improper lane usage, driving without registration, and no proof of insurance. If you don't pay your fine or appear in court at the time appointed, your horse-driving license will be suspended." The Sheriff tipped his hat to Samson and Delilah and galloped off in a cloud of dust, with Tonto riding by his side. Samson and Delilah stared in astonishment, as the sheriff yelled out "Hi ho Silver" in the distance. "The William Tell Overture" was playing, but Samson wasn't sure where it was coming from.

"Who was that masked man?" Delilah asked.

"Some asshole," Samson said. He and Delilah tore up the tickets, threw them away, and still wild and free, rode off into the sunset.

Chapter 17
Bullworth

"The majority is always wrong."
—**Henrik Ibsen**

"There's a lot of money in poverty."
—**Howard Dickstein**

Stein came up close to Samson and hollered in his ear, "Mr. Samson!"

Samson awoke from the daydream with a start, looked around, and sat up straight in his chair.

"If you don't pay your taxes, Mr. Samson, the rest of us have to pay more," Stein said.

"How do you figure?"

"Obviously, if you don't pay, everybody else has to make up for your share."

"That's obvious to you, is it?"

"Obviously it's obvious."

"So you think I have a share," Samson said.

"Of course. Everybody has to pay their fair share."

"So let me get this straight, Mr. Stein," Samson rejoined. "Everybody's assigned a share of the taxes. And when you get to the bottom line of your tax return, you say to yourself, 'Well, old Samson over there isn't paying any tax, so I think I'll pay extra to cover his share'?"

"No, of course not."

"So that disposes of that argument."

"Wait, huh? I don't—"

"It's a spurious argument," Samson interrupted. "It's totally false to say that if some people don't pay taxes other people have to pay more. If I don't pay my taxes it has no effect at all on what you pay or what someone else pays. It just means the government has less money to waste. And more money is left in the productive private sector, stimulating the growth of businesses who can then hire more people, creating jobs and economic expansion. So if I don't pay my taxes, it doesn't hurt anybody else; it *helps* them. This is Economics 101. Maybe you were absent that day."

"And maybe you think it's fair that everyone else should have to pay taxes except you" Stein argued.

"No, I don't think they should have to pay either."

"So you're not willing to pay your share to help the poor?"

"Do you actually know any poor people, Mr. Stein?"

Stein hesitated. " Uh, I, uh—"

"See, the reason you love the poor so much is because you never met any."

"Don't you care about the poor?" Stein asked.

"They aren't that great."

"So you don't care what happens to the homeless?"

"You mean those drunks who piss in the street? Do *you* care what happens to them?"

"Yeah, I do!"

"Well, then why don't you invite them to come live at your place?"

Samson was taking a risk with this tack. In a world where social norms require us to show compassion for the poor and downtrodden, his insouciant attitude could be perceived by the jury as showing a lack of compassion. In a liberal social order, compassion is considered the paramount virtue. And some of the jurors were appalled at Samson's forthright apathy to the plight of the poor. On the other hand, some jurors were holding back laughter and snickers at his irreverence toward the sacrosanct shibboleths of the welfare state. During jury selection Samson had succeeded in getting some people on the jury who he felt would understand his point of view. He figured he didn't need all the jurors on his side, just enough to assure that there weren't twelve votes for conviction. And besides, it wasn't his style to pull his punches or conceal who he was.

"You're real compassionate, aren't you, Samson?" Stein asked.

"No, Mr. Stein, I'm not compassionate like you and Elliott Mess. Steal people's money, punch them in the face, threaten them with guns, seize their homes, close their businesses, put their employees out of work, take everything they have, destroy their lives, and throw them in jail. That's your idea of compassion."

"Move to strike, your honor."

The judge turned to the jury. "Sustained. The jury will disregard everything Mr. Samson said."

"Why should they disregard it, your honor? It's all true. These people hide behind this word 'compassion.' What they do has nothing to do with compassion. It's all about money and power and—"

"Mr. Samson," the judge interrupted. "You are out of order, and in contempt! If another word comes out of your mouth, I'm going to have your bail revoked, and have these guards handcuff you and put you right back in jail. You got that?"

Samson stopped talking. But looking over at the jury he got the feeling that some of the jurors had wanted to hear him finish and weren't happy to see him silenced. *Score that round for me*, he thought. He was beginning to feel that he was heading for at least a hung jury. And maybe even acquittal.

Dubious Philosophical Musings
Tangentially Related to the Story

Part II
The Paradox of Capitalism

"Capitalism has worked very well. Anyone who wants to move to North Korea is welcome."
—Bill Gates

"If you put the federal government in charge of the Sahara Desert, in five years there'd be a shortage of sand."
—Milton Friedman

It's a paradox. Capitalism has been a dazzling success. It has raised billions of people out of the physical privation which was the lot of human beings since our species emerged from the trees half a million years ago. Only in the last two centuries, thanks to capitalism, have we raised ourselves into the material opulence of modern civilization. Yet despite its spectacular record of economic achievement, capitalism is unpopular. The masses, who have been liberated by capitalism's wealth creating power from centuries of privation and oppression, are largely oblivious to the source of their well being. That's why voters are easily persuaded by demogogues to jettison capitalism in favor of collectivist economic policies with an horrendous track record, thereby violating a basic axiom of common sense: If it ain't broke, don't fix it.

For 500,000 years, most humans lived like animals under subsistence conditions that modern-day Americans (like those reading this book) would have found insufferable. Our ancestors were cold when it got cold, hot when it got hot, wet when it rained, and chronically worried about whether they'd have enough food to make it through the winter. If they got sick or injured all they could do was suffer until they got better or died. If they got a toothache there was no relief. They lived in caves, tepees, or dirty little shacks, under horribly unsanitary conditions, with no heat, light, plumbing, electricity, or furniture. They rarely bathed and never brushed their teeth. They stank. They had little entertainment, had to go outside in the cold to relieve themselves, and were lucky if they lived to the age of 40.

In the last 200 years all this has changed. As a result of technological innovation an extraordinary amount of material wealth has been created and widely disbursed among the populations of advanced post industrial countries. Thanks to the inventions of the last 200 years, ordinary people in America, Europe, and much of Asia and South America, have a standard of living today far higher than the King of England had in the 1700s. The average American has central heat in the winter, and air conditioning in the summer. He can speak to anyone anywhere in the world by pushing a few buttons. He can go to a supermarket and take his pick of 50,000 food items from around the world. And he can fly anywhere in the world and be there the next day. With a push of a button he can get instant access to limitless information or entertainment of his choosing. He has hot running water and indoor toilets, medical treatment for most maladies, electric power, cars, dishwashers, washing machines, vacuum cleaners, TVs, radios, and computers. None of these amenities was available to the Roman Emperor or the Kings of Europe.

What has produced this cornucopia of wealth? Capitalism. The free enterprise system unleashes creativity and inspires genius that has generated the discoveries and inventions that have transformed human life. The age of capitalism enabled Edison to harness electricity, Alexander Graham Bell to invent the telephone, the Wright Brothers to create human flight, Ford to manufacture cars, Salk to discover the polio vaccine, and Steve Jobs to usher in the age of the personal computer. Without capitalism we'd all still be hungry, shivering in our shacks, ignorant, and miserable.

And how do the masses in modern democracies show their appreciation of the beneficence capitalism has bestowed upon them? They vote against it. Not consciously of course, not for candidates who forthrightly declare what they really believe. When was the last time you heard a politician say, "I'm a socialist, and I want to dismantle the free enterprise system that has produced our prosperity. I want the government to over-regulate or nationalize the businesses that create the wealth you all enjoy, and gradually turn this into a socialist country, where you won't be allowed to blow your nose without getting permission from bureaucrats, and you'll be dependent on government for your sustenance"? No, politicians don't ever say that. But that's what they do. And we, the people, re-elect them.

Chapter 18
Enemy of the State

"The most dangerous man to any government is the man who is able to think things out... without regard to the prevailing superstitions and taboos. Almost inevitably he comes to the conclusion that the government he lives under is dishonest, insane, intolerable."
—H. L. Mencken

"Something's rotten in the state of Denmark."
—William Shakespeare

The Plan for Universal Compliance included Canons of Ethics to guide IRS agents, and more particularly Special Agents, toward achieving the Plan's goals of full compliance with the code, total national control, and ultimately, world rule, while maintaining the highest ethical standards. The ethical bar was set high. The IRS Canons of Ethics included the following provision, difficult to understand because it's written in bureaucratese:

Limitations on Procedural Intervention in Criminal Cases Arising Under the Code. Extraordinary interposition, intervention, or other intercession by Special Agents is permis-

> sible in the criminal procedure of those accused of income tax evasion, failure to file a tax return, tax fraud, or other prosecutions arising under the Code, or related Federal criminal statutes, only when circumstances make it appear likely, in the judgment of IRS or other Treasury Department Managers, that, in the absence of such interposition, intervention, or other intercession, conviction is either unlikely, or the outcome of the pending procedure is otherwise inconsistent with optimal enforcement of the Code, and attainment of broader objectives of the Agency, viewed within the context of the Plan for Universal Compliance (PUC).

If you don't understand all that obscure pseudo-legalistic blather, don't feel bad; that just means you're a normal person. Translated into regular language, it means that special agents are only permitted to rig trials in order to get a conviction if it looks like the guy would otherwise get off. And in such cases special agents are required to get approval to rig the trial from higher ups at the agency. The application of the intervention policy was subject to interpretation in light of catch 23.

Elliott Mess could see that Samson's trial wasn't going according to plan. He applied for permission for intervention on an expedited basis, and the Plan for Universal Compliance being extraordinarily efficient for a government program, he received approval from the regional supervisor (his father) the same day. The most common method of "intervention" was entitled, also in bureaucratese, "mandatory forensic trier of fact re-indoctrination and national service subordination." To regular folks this type of intervention is indistinguishable from, um, jury tampering, which is a felony if you or I do it, but under the Plan, was permitted for IRS special agents.

Samson was walking down the hallway toward the courtroom, when he caught Elliott Mess in the act of "mandatory forensic trier of fact re-indoctrination and national service subordination." There was Mess talking secretively to juror # 1 outside the door to the jury room. Samson, as yet unseen by Mess, stopped in his tracks, then spotted a water fountain. He went to it and bent over, pretending to drink, so he could observe what was going on without being noticed. Juror #1 looked shaken.

When Mess was done mandatorily re-indoctrinating and subordinating him, the poor fellow re-entered the jury room. Mess followed him to the edge of the door, beckoned to someone with his finger and then came back out into the hall with his hand on the shoulder of juror #2. He mandatorily re-indoctrinated and subordinated juror #2 for several minutes. As he talked to these jurors he seemed to be standing unnaturally close to them. As juror #2, also looking shaken, went back into the jury room, Mess noticed Samson eyeing him. Samson walked up to Mess aggressively, and got right in his face like an angry baseball manager to an umpire. "What the hell do you think you're doing?" he shouted, his mouth only inches from Mess's nose. "I'll get a mistrial. The next one on trial will be *you!*"

Mess backed off calmly, putting some distance between the two men. "Your trouble is you don't know when you're licked, Samson. Maybe after a few years in prison, you'll figure out how it works." Mess turned to walk away, but Samson moved closer to him menacingly, blocking his path, both his fists clenched. Mess made no move to defend himself. He nonchalantly put his hands in his pockets. He turned back squarely to face Samson, making his undefended face an easy target.

"Go ahead," he said quietly. "I'll have the judge revoke your bail release and put you in a nasty little prison with Zachariah Moussaui, the Unabomber, and the other lunatics." Samson closed his eyes as if counting to ten to calm down, unclenched his fists, backed off, and turned to walk away. It was clear he would need a new strategy.

Chapter 19
David and Goliath

*"The surest way to destroy the basis of existing society
is through debasement of the currency.
And the process is accomplished in a manner that
not one man in a hundred can understand."*
—John Maynard Keynes

*"You used to be so amused at Napoleon in rags and the
language that he used. Go to him now, he calls you, you can't
refuse. When you got nothing, you got nothing to lose."*
—Bob Dylan

Samson had been taught the used car business years earlier by Morris Greenstein, an old German Jew and holocaust survivor. Samson had been broke at the time. He came into Greenstein's car lot, looking for a cheap car. Greenstein was so impressed with Samson's natural bargaining skills that he offered him a job as manager on the spot. He was getting old and was happy to have an ambitious young guy help him run the business.

Samson was a quick study. He came up with some clever marketing ideas and other improvements to the business that quickly added to the bottom line. Although Greenstein was like a second father to Samson, there was always a bit of an edge to their relationship. Greenstein made Samson a partner, and a few years later Samson bought Greenstein out. Unfortunately, they got into a dispute about the terms of the buyout and almost got into a lawsuit, leaving them with ambiguous feelings toward each other.

Samson wasn't really crazy about the idea of going to his old mentor for help, and he thought Greenstein would probably turn him down. But when Greenstein got wind of what had happened to Samson, he had called, and offered his condolences. Samson didn't see any other way out of the fix he was in.

Greenstein lived in an old-fashioned brick home that was large enough to be considered a mansion. Samson was let in by Greenstein's housekeeper and shown to an office that reminded him of Don Corleone's in *The Godfather*. Greenstein was in his mid-eighties but still sharp. He was seated behind his desk in a swivel chair. He had white hair and was wearing a white suit. He spoke with a German accent with a Yiddish inflection. Samson thought of him as a cross between a Mafia don and a rabbi. Samson stood in front of Greenstein's desk shifting on his feet. "So what do you want, Morris? I know you didn't call me here to help me."

"Actually, you got me wrong, Sam. I *did* call you here to help you."

"Okay, great. Congressman Les Moore says he'll get me out of this for a hundred and fifty thousand dollars."

Greenstein paused, leaned back in his chair and put his hands behind his head. "You want I should lend you a hundred and fifty thousand dollars?"

"Well, it'll keep me out of jail. And y'know, ask around the neighborhood about me; I know how to return a favor."

"You took that line from Vito Corleone."

"Yeah okay, so he said it first."

"After all the times you screwed me, now you want I should lend you money?"

"I screwed you. You screwed me. We both made money."

Greenstein laughed. "Okay, here's the deal," he said. "I'll lend you the money on two conditions." He paused as Samson sat down. "First, don't pay off the crooked congressman."

"Huh?"

"Don't pay off the crooked congressman," Greenstein repeated.

"I don't get it. If I don't pay off the congressman, what's the point?"

"Look, I know Les Moore," Greenstein said. "That stupid bastard'll take your money, and won't do a damn thing for you."

"Okay, so what do you want me to do?"

"I want you to destroy them."

"Who? You want me to destroy who?"

"The IRS."

There was a pause during which Samson stared vacantly at Greenstein, as if trying to comprehend the incomprehensible. He peered into Greenstein's eyes searching for some vestige of sanity. He waited for Greenstein to continue to find out if maybe it was a joke, or if there might be some qualifier to bring the idea back within the bounds of reality. When he realized that no further explanation was coming, he said, "You've lost it, Morris."

"That's my condition."

"You want me to destroy the IRS."

Greenstein nodded. Samson shrugged his shoulders in disbelief. "That's insane," he said.

Greenstein leaned forward in his chair, as if he didn't want anyone else to hear him. "If you don't, you're gonna lose."

"What the hell are you talking about, Morris?"

"It's okay to be a greedy sonofabitch—as long as it works. But it's not working, Sam."

"So what do you want me to do?"

"Save the country."

Samson got up out of his seat, paced back and forth, then went toward the door as if he were going to leave. He stood there for a moment reflecting on his options: go to prison, or deal with Greenstein. He went back and sat down.

"You want me to save the country."

"Yeah."

"Save it from what?"

"You know damn well what."

"And what makes you think the country wants me to save it?" As he said this, Samson recognized how silly it sounded.

"It doesn't."

"Uh-huh."

"It's a long shot."

"It's not a long shot; it's impossible!" Samson stood up and again began pacing the floor. In the past few months his perception of the world in which he was living had undergone wrenching changes. Now this. Anything seemed possible as he began to come to grips with the implications of Greenstein's mind-bending proposal. Samson had been endowed by nature with natural self-confidence, but he had always believed in going for goals that were attainable. He might try to put together a million-dollar deal but not a billion-dollar deal, because it was out of his league, at least at this stage in his career. By the same token it seemed to him that for a broke used car dealer facing criminal charges to try to destroy the IRS seemed a tad out of his league. He came to a standstill in front of Greenstein's desk. "Remember, Morris, when you were teaching me the business, what you said: 'I can't sleep at night unless I've screwed at least one person during the day.'? If I'm a greedy sonofabitch, I learned it from you."

"Look, Sam, how long did it take you to make your first million dollars?"

"Five years."

"And how long did it take them to take every penny?"

"Five minutes."

"So what do you think is going on?"

"I don't know."

"Do you think you're the only one this is happening to? This is going on all around the country. They're coming down hard. You're not playing with some petty tyrants in the bureaucracy anymore. You're an enemy of the state. And they'll squash you like a gnat. You need to get off the defensive. Take the conflict to a whole new level. You're David against Goliath. But if you succeed, you'll be a hero, like Abraham Lincoln, Mahatma Gandhi, Martin Luther King."

"They all got shot."

"We all have a cross to bear."

"I don't *wanna* get shot."

"You think those guys wanted to get shot? You're laughing. Look, Sam. I've seen this before in Germany. I was just a kid; I couldn't fight back. My whole family died in the holocaust. This isn't just about you. You're young and strong. You gotta fight back, Sam. Otherwise, they're gonna get universal compliance with the code."

At these ominously familiar words Samson's eyes opened wide. He leaned on the desk with both hands staring at Greenstein. "I've heard that before."

"What?"

"Universal compliance with the code. In a dream. No, it wasn't just in the dream. The IRS supervisor said it."

"Then you know what's going to happen to us, Samson, not just to you, to our people, to all of us, unless you destroy the Philistines."

"Why me?"

"Come on, Sam. You always knew you had something more important to do with your life than selling junkers." Greenstein got up and walked over to his bookshelf. He removed some books, revealing a wall safe. He dialed the combination, opened the safe, counted out a stack of bills, and closed the safe. He walked back behind the desk, still holding the cash, which Samson, still standing, was eyeing.

"You said there were two conditions," Samson said. "Destroy the IRS. And what's the other one?"

"Pay me back double."

"Of course."

Greenstein handed Samson the cash. Samson stuffed it in his pockets and left.

The next day was Saturday so court wasn't in session. Samson went to Synagogue for the first time since his bar mitzvah thirty years earlier; he wasn't sure why. After the service, he went to meet Buddha for lunch at the Cadillac Cafe.

. . .

They sat at the same booth where Delilah and Buddha had sat before. They spoke quietly, not wanting to be overheard.

"It's crazy, Sam," Buddha responded after Samson told him what he was thinking. "They'll kill you. Morris Greenstein has lost his marbles. Just take the money, get out of the country, and don't look back."

"Look, Buddha, my whole life," Samson said, "I never did nothin' for nobody."

"So? Why change now?"

"They declared war on me. I'm just fighting back. You need to choose sides, Buddha."

"You know I wanna be on your side—if I thought we had a chance to pull it off. But who are you kidding? You think you're gonna go to war against the United States government? I'm not willing to go back to prison, Sam."

"What about Delilah?"

"Hasn't she done enough?" Buddha asked, incredulous that Samson had to ask. *The estrogen effect*, no doubt, he thought. Was Samson so blinded by "love" or "lust" or heartache or whatever, that even after everything that had happened he still hadn't figured out Delilah couldn't be trusted? Or was his judgment diminished by his desperate circumstances?

Buddha's situation was painfully conflicted, as he weighed the competing demands of his loyalty to Samson, against his aversion to going back to prison. He was trying to resolve this dilemma by appearing to cooperate with the IRS, while at the same time not giving them any information that would actually help them get a conviction against Samson. In any event, he rationalized, if Samson was right that they were rigging his trial, conviction was a foregone conclusion, and his testimony wouldn't change the outcome.

Dubious Philosophical Musings

Part III
Democracy

"In the lexicon of the political class, the word 'sacrifice' means that the citizens are supposed to mail even more of their income to Washington so that the political class will not have to sacrifice the pleasure of spending it."
—George Will

"Under capitalism, man exploits man. Under communism, it's just the opposite."
—John Kenneth Galbraith

The definition of democracy is "idiots voting." Okay, that's an oversimplification. Let me put it this way. The level of sophistication of voters runs the gamut from the Yale political science professor who does a cost benefit analysis of candidates' stands on 178 issues, to some nincompoop at the other end of the sophistication spectrum, the "low information voter," who votes for the guy with the nicest tie. Some voters are so dumb that they vote for a candidate because he comes up with a cool slogan, like, say, "Hope and Change." Millions of voters decide not to vote for a candidate because his opponent runs a 30-second spot saying the guy was mean to his dog.

Now if you wonder where on the voter sophistication continuum you fall, here's a hint: If you're influenced by political ads, you're there at the dumb end of the continuum next to the guy who votes for the candidate who isn't mean to his dog. If you're so uninformed that you're influenced by political ads, and you care about your country, do your patriotic duty: Don't vote.

Many voters don't have a clue about basic principles of political economics. They fail to recognize the severe damage that's been done to our free enterprise system by the "reforms" introduced, one at a time, over the past hundred years, all in the name of wonderful sounding causes like consumer protection, helping the needy, environmentalism, social justice, fairness, universal healthcare, paying down the debt, redistributing wealth, or any other cause concocted by politicians making promises about all the "free" stuff they're going to give you if you vote for them, with no explanation about who will pay for it. Why are voters so gullible? So eager to embrace new policies to "improve" the free enterprise system by expanding government power, or creating more "free" government give away programs? Why do they vote for candidates who impose anti-growth regulations on business, increase government spending, create new bureaucracies, raise taxes, and incur more public debt? These policies make the government bigger, and the wealth producing private sector correspondingly smaller, which in turn makes all of us poorer. See, the free stuff isn't really free. You have to pay for it. How hard is it to understand that? So why are these wealth destroying, anti-capitalist policies so popular?

Because capitalism is imperfect. If unfettered capitalism produced utopia, and everybody were happy, who would want to change it? The capitalist system grows out of human nature, and human nature is imperfect. The people have become accustomed to the wealth created by capitalism and take it for granted, on the theory that whoever discovered water, it sure wasn't a fish. They think that prosperity is their birthright; that the wealth of nations is just there, like the environment. A large portion of the public doesn't understand the causal link between capitalism and prosperity; when they look at capitalism, what they see are its flaws. They think government intervention will improve the economic system. But it never does.

If you fundamentally transform the goose that laid the golden egg, it doesn't cause the goose to spread the eggs around more equitably; it causes the goose to stop laying eggs. Equality can be achieved only by making everyone equally poor. Yet the masses pursue the illusion, fostered by politicians and ideologues, that because capitalism is imperfect, we should try some alternative. It turns out, however, that although capitalism is imperfect, the alternative is worse.

Futile efforts to create a perfect political economic system are a testament to a positive human trait; we strive for perfection. The problem is that as long as human beings are imperfect, our social institutions will also be imperfect. We can't solve the problem of our own imperfect nature by making our institutions perfect. And this is why all utopian social theories fail when put into practice. If the free enterprise system is compared to some Platonic ideal, it comes up short. But in the real world the only alternative to capitalism is some variation of socialism. And the problem with socialism is that it sucks. Whether it's the iron curtain Soviet/

Stalinist variety or European style "socialism light," they both suck. Any attempts to improve on the flaws of capitalism, or achieve social perfection through social policy, are doomed to failure. As Woody Allen put it, "Political solutions don't work."

If you want perfection, try achieving it on a personal spiritual level, as suggested by teachers like Jesus and Buddha. That might actually work. Attempts to achieve perfection via social engineering and political activism don't work, and they tend to wreak havoc.

Chapter 20
The Ides of March

"We learn from history that we do not learn from history."
—Friedrich Wilhelm Hegel

"You say you are my friend. But when I was down, you just stood there grinning."
—Bob Dylan

Early Monday morning, Elliott Mess sat behind his desk. Delilah and Buddha sat across from him. Buddha bit his lip. He was tense. He picked up his briefcase, laid it down on the desk, and removed stacks of Spoilsport Motors financial records and a couple of CDs. As Buddha looked through the papers, Delilah stood up and gestured to Mess, pointing to the door. "Elliott, can I talk to you in private for a minute?" she asked flirtatiously.

Mess eyed Buddha suspiciously, not sure he should leave him alone in the office. He knew Buddha had divided loyalties and was aware of his history of cybercrime, but figured he wouldn't have the nerve to try anything right there under Mess's nose. Seeing Buddha engrossed in the pile of papers, he followed Delilah out into the hall. As soon as they were out the door Buddha quickly came round to the front of the desk, sat down, slipped a DVD out of his pocket, and put it in the computer. He typed frantically, looking up frequently to make sure Mess wasn't coming back in. When he was done, he took out the disk and put it back in his pocket, and went back to his chair on the other side of the desk, just as Delilah and Mess came back in the office..

Mess eyed Buddha suspiciously.

...

Later that morning the trial resumed. During the lunchtime recess, Samson was in the lobby of the courthouse on his cell phone. "I'll wire you ten percent today as a deposit, and pay the rest in cash when I get there," he said. When he hung up, he made another call. When the person he was calling answered, Samson asked, "Is it ready? Okay, give me the account number and routing number." He wrote the information on a small note pad. "Is there anything else I need to do? I can't be certain exactly when, but I think it will arrive tomorrow, or the next day, if all goes well. Okay, good, thanks."

Delilah walked by. Samson hung up the phone and caught up with her. He put his arm around her and whispered in her ear. She flirted with him, but when Mess came into view, she walked away from Samson and entered the courtroom with Mess.

Knowing that the outcome of the trial was predetermined gave Samson a degree of detachment about the whole process. Buddha was on the witness stand, being examined by Stein.

After asking a few routine questions, Stein asked Buddha, "As Mr. Samson's bookkeeper, was it your job to prepare tax returns?"

"Tax returns? For Sam Samson?" Buddha replied. "Are you kidding?"

"I don't kid," Stein said.

"Sam didn't pay taxes."

"Did you ever file a tax return for Mr. Samson or his business?"

"Yeah, last year I filed a tax return showing income of fourteen thousand dollars."

"Fourteen thousand dollars income for the year? Was that accurate?"

"It would be accurate if you added a zero. And then doubled your answer."

"So let's see. If you add a zero, that would take the fourteen thousand up to one hundred forty thousand. And if you double it, that would bring it up to two hundred eighty thousand dollars. Is that correct?"

"Yeah, that's correct."

"So just to be clear, you're saying that Sam Samson made two hundred eighty thousand dollars profit last year, not the fourteen thousand he reported on his tax return."

"Yeah, that's what I'm saying."

"And to make sure there's no misunderstanding here, sir, you're talking about the net profit of his used car business, not gross revenues."

"Yes, net profit, correct. The gross sales figure was much higher."

"Okay, well, just to put this in context, what were the gross sales figures for the year?"

"It was over two point six million in auto sales, plus an additional eighty-two thousand dollars in dealer fees and miscellaneous income. That goes right to the bottom line because there's no cost of sales involved."

"Okay, so the number two hundred eighty thousand is the net profit? The amount of money Mr. Samson actually put in his pocket? His take-home pay?"

"Correct."

"And did you pay any federal taxes for Mr. Samson or his business?"

"No. Sam told me not to."

"Thank you. Your witness."

Stein looked over at the jury confidently as he walked to the counsel table and sat down. Samson hesitated for a moment. The judge began tapping her fingers on the bench, indicating her impatience. Samson stood up, but moved slowly, as if lost in thought at how to respond to this betrayal. Elliott Mess sat next to Delilah, his arm casually resting on the back of her seat, touching her. He whispered in her ear and she giggled. Samson saw this but ignored it.

Samson's cross-examination was short, and not at all to the point. "You too, Buddha?" he asked, and sat down. What was the point in going any further?

Chapter 21
Profiles in Courage

"There are people who occasionally stumble upon the truth. But usually they manage to pick themselves up, dust themselves off, and continue on their way as if nothing had happened."
—Winston Churchill

"Show them the light and they will follow it anywhere."
—Firesign Theater

Stein rested his case, figuring that Buddha's devastating testimony clinched the outcome. The judge gave Samson the chance to put on his case, but he had apparently given up as he declined to present any defense. So Stein stood up in front of the jury to give his closing argument.

"Sam Samson," Stein began, "says it's his patriotic duty to lie, cheat, and refuse to pay one nickel of the costs of running our government. He says he decided to give himself a tax cut. A tax cut! Do you buy that? See, in a democracy, Mr. Samson, you don't get to make that decision. That's up to Congress. Now Mr. Samson doesn't mind enjoying the benefits of American citizenship, to drive on our roads, be protected by our national defense, or enjoy our freedoms, freedoms which allowed him to make a lot of money. He wants the benefits; he just doesn't want to help pay for it.

"Of course Sam Samson isn't the only one who doesn't want to pay taxes. He represents an entire class of selfish, greedy people who get rich at everyone else's expense, and then refuse to pay their fair share of the costs of America's social infrastructure. Mr. Samson says the government wastes money and makes the tired old argument heard from anti-government extremists that taxes are robbery. But do you believe that? The income tax is egalitarian. Those at the top are supposed to pay the most because they can afford to, and those at the bottom are supposed to receive benefits because they are in need. Everyone who can afford to has to pay - except for tax cheaters like Mr. Samson. Now Mr. Samson believes that he's too good to have to suffer with the rest of us. But if you acquit him, other people will think they too can get away without paying taxes. Without funding, our government will fall apart and we'll have chaos.

"There's a word for what Sam Samson believes. It's called 'anarchy.' If no one pays taxes you have no government. And that's what you get. If you want to see what anarchy looks like we have many historical examples, all of which involve gangs of warlords battling it out in the streets with AK 47s. Lebanon, Chechnya, Serbia, Croatia, Somalia, Libya, Afghanistan. Get the idea? Now the U.S. government may not be perfectly efficient, but our system of government has created the most prosperous, most successful civilization in history. Tax cheaters like Sam Samson, would destroy that civilization by destroying the government that makes it possible.

"Mr. Samson says he's opposed to taxes. But he's not opposed to taxes for you and me. He's just opposed to taxes for himself." Stein sat down, proud of his brief but pithy closing.

"Mr. Samson," said the judge.

Samson stood up. He looked back at Elliott Mess who stared at him vacantly. He took his time walking over in front of the jury box. Before he started speaking he walked the length of the jury box looking each juror in the eyes. Then he looked back at Delilah, who smiled at him until she saw Mess looking at her. Then she averted her gaze. Samson turned back to the jury.

"When I was a boy growing up in Philadelphia," he began, "my father was a hard-working immigrant who taught me that America was the home of freedom, a place where anyone who was willing to work hard could fulfill their dreams and find success. But that America is gone. In business I learned that you can't blow your nose without some government bureaucrat telling you it's against the law.

"And then there are the taxes. Corporate taxes, income taxes, Social Security taxes, Medicare taxes, payroll taxes, workers comp, unemployment, state corporate taxes, state income taxes, sales taxes, county taxes, city taxes, property taxes, and public transportation taxes. If you pay all those taxes, you don't have any money left to run your business, and you go out of business."

Stein stood up. "Your honor, I object to this entire speech; it's all irrelevant. We're not here to debate Mr. Samson's views on public tax policy, only whether he violated the law."

"I'm going to allow it, Mr. Stein. He has a lot of latitude on closing argument. And he's obviously guilty as hell, so what are you worried about?"

Stein sat down. Samson thanked the judge for her impartiality, and then continued to the jury: "The taxes have become so burdensome that millions of ordinary people routinely cheat: taxi drivers, waitresses, gardeners, handymen, hairdressers—anyone who's paid in cash. So what happened to me could just as easily happen to your brother-in-law, your sister, your cousins, or your aunts—or to you. But we regular folks get into trouble if we don't pay taxes. If you want to get away with not paying taxes, you have to be a high level government official. I already mentioned Senate Majority Leader Tom Daschle. But Congressman Charles Rangel, chairman of the House Ways and Means Committee, also cheated on taxes. Elliott Mess never showed up on his doorstep. In fact, even the secretary of the treasury himself, the federal agency which oversees the Internal Revenue Service. That's right, Treasury Secretary Timothy Geithner, Elliott Mess's boss, cheated on taxes. And nothing happened to him."

Stein stood up again and raised his hand. "Your honor, I object. These men aren't on trial. These allegations are irrelevant and aren't in evidence."

"These stories about top-level politicians cheating on taxes have been all over the news," Samson replied. "And it may seem irrelevant to you, Mr. Stein, that the secretary of the treasury is a tax cheat, but I'll bet the jury doesn't think it's irrelevant."

"Objection sustained!" said the judge, pounding her gavel. "I'm the one who decides what's relevant, Mr. Samson, and you are not to mention the names of any other government officials who cheat on taxes. The jury will disregard Mr. Samson's remarks."

"Sure they will, your honor," Samson said. The jury was *not* disregarding Samson's remarks. "I won't mention any more government officials who cheat on taxes." Samson turned to Mess. "So, Elliott, do you have one of those devices to erase the memories of the jurors, y'know, like Tommy Lee Jones and Will Smith used in 'Men in Black,' so they won't remember about all the big shot government officials who cheat on taxes even though we commoners aren't allowed to?"

"Mr. Samson!" the judge scolded.

"Okay, never mind," Samson said. "Let's talk about something else. The 'persecuting' attorney. Now Phil S. Stein says that I'm an anarchist. And he presents us with an unpleasant choice. We have to choose, he tells us, between two extremes. Either we accept the notion of a vast over-reaching government bureaucracy that extends its control over every aspect of our lives, funded by a ruthless tax collection agency that runs roughshod over our rights, or we can choose the opposite—no government at all. And he conjures up images of warlords with AK 47s in Somalia and Afghanistan, promulgating violence, anarchy, and chaos. Stark choice. But in America do we really have to choose between these two extremes: either an oppressive government where jack-booted IRS agents steal our money, seize our homes, and throw us in jail, or the opposite extreme of anarchy in our streets?

"Mr. Stein is apparently unaware that there is a third choice, a middle way between these two extremes of anarchy or tyranny. It's called freedom. The freedom our Founding Fathers created when they wrote our amazing constitution, based on the concept of limited government. The freedom our great-grandparents still enjoyed a hundred years ago, before the creation of the modern bureaucratic state controlled by Washington. Today we no longer have limited government. We have government without limit. The concept of limited government, the foundation of personal freedom, has been overthrown by people like Phil S. Stein, and Elliott Mess, and the greedy, crooked politicians for whom they work.

"In the old days, in the time of our great-grandparents, America had no IRS. We didn't need an IRS because the government was small and didn't need much money. I'm not an anarchist. I never said we shouldn't have a government. Freedom is possible when government is the right size. Mr. Stein is correct that if there is *no* government, you have anarchy and warlords and chaos. But what about the opposite extreme, where there's *too* much government? Is that how you want to live? Under a huge government bureaucracy that regulates your business, your bank accounts, your property; invades your privacy, forces you to buy government-approved health insurance, monitors your movement with radar and video cameras and drones, spies on your financial transactions, tells you how to live, and wastes trillions of dollars of *your* money, running thousands of government agencies, most of which are either useless or harmful, and overrun with corruption, fraud, and abuse?

"Did you know our original Constitution didn't permit an income tax? And we didn't have anarchy in our streets and warlords with machine guns. We had prosperity and growth. That was the golden age of America. Do you know why our Founding Fathers didn't want an income tax? Thomas Jefferson, the author of the Declaration of Independence, said that extravagant government spending leads to public debt, that 'taxation follows that, and in its train wretchedness and oppression.' Sound familiar? Extravagant government spending, then high taxes, wretchedness, and oppression; we know all about that today. Our Founding Fathers thought an income tax was oppressive. They didn't want government officials probing into our finances and extracting money from us by force. And they didn't want the government to have an unlimited source of money, funded on the backs of the people. They opposed an income tax because they knew where it would lead—to the huge government bureaucracy like the one we all live under today.

"And speaking of the Constitution, what about the 4th amendment? 'The right of the people to be secure in their persons, papers, houses, and effects, against unreasonable searches and seizures, *shall not be violated!*' And the 5th amendment: 'No person ... shall be deprived of life, liberty, or property without due process of law.' What does that mean, 'due process of law'? I'll tell you what it meant to our Founding Fathers. It meant the government couldn't just decide to take everything you have and throw you in jail. If the government thought you owed them money, 'due process of law' meant they had to go into court and prove it first—*before* they took everything you own. That's what 'due process of law' means. So what do you think? Do you feel safe and secure? Do you think that in America today these constitutional amendments protect you from arbitrary abuse of power by the government?

"No, they don't. Because the IRS doesn't worry about little things like due process of law and the Bill of Rights. If someone else claims you owe them money, they have to take you to court and prove it. But not the IRS. They just come and take your house. And then they just throw you in jail. Which is what they did to me. Didn't we get rid of the barbarity of debtors prison hundreds of years ago? Unless you're the IRS.

They're still running debtors' prisons. See, they think the Constitution doesn't apply to them.

"As I said, the original Constitution didn't include an income tax. A hundred years ago, the 16th amendment created the income tax. It says 'Congress shall have the power to lay and collect taxes on incomes from whatever source derived.' But where does it say that they can put you in jail for not paying taxes? Why can't they collect taxes using ordinary means like other creditors? They can garnish your wages, seize your property, or your bank accounts. Isn't that enough? Why jail? Putting people in jail for not paying their debts is an unconstitutional instrument of intimidation and oppression by a tyrannical government agency. There is no place for debtors' prisons in a free country.

"See, our Founding Fathers didn't think free men should live in fear of the government. But today can any one of you honestly say that you're not afraid of the IRS? If you're not afraid, stand up now! Because the last protection of our rights in a free society is the right to trial by a jury of our peers. The jury can protect each of us from oppressive government by refusing to enforce oppressive laws, by refusing to unjustly convict your fellow citizens. When government thugs start tampering with juries, we lose what's left of our freedom. So don't be afraid. Tell the judge what's going on! Tell her what Elliott Mess did!"

So saying, Samson pointed his finger accusingly at Mess, as if he were the one on trial. Stein leaped to his feet, pounded the table, and raised his hand high over his head. Elliott Mess stopped whispering to Delilah and sat up, alert on the edge of his seat, staring coldly at Samson.

"Your honor, I object!' Stein shouted.

"Mr. Samson!" the judge shouted.

Samson ignored her. He pounded the banister in front of the jury box with his fist.

"Stand up, tell her! Don't let this happen in America!"

The judge pounded her gavel. But before she could give Samson hell, juror #1, suddenly, but timidly, stood up. The other jurors looked up at him expectantly and began whispering among themselves, hoping that he would be the one to stick his neck out. Everyone else in the courtroom was silent, stunned.

Juror #1 spoke nervously. "Your honor, I-I, uh, have to tell you something important."

Mess signaled to a large, scary looking IRS agent in the back of the room, who quickly came up to him. Mess whispered in his ear, then looked back at juror #1 calmly and stared him down. The other IRS agent also stared at juror #1 coldly, then began dialing on his cell phone, and heading slowly for the door. Juror #1 got flustered and looked away.

The judge was oblivious to what was going on. "What is it?" she said impatiently to juror # 1.

"I...uh...I...uh," juror #1 stammered.

"Spit it out," she said. "What do you want?"

"I need to use the rest room."

Mess signaled to the other agent, who put down the cell phone, and moved back to his seat.

"Can it wait until Mr. Samson finishes his closing?" she asked in an exasperated tone.

"Yes, your honor."

The judge rolled her eyes. Juror #1 sat down. The woman juror sitting next to him patted him on his arm reassuringly.

Samson paced up and down in front of the jury imploringly, looking for someone else with the courage to stand up.

"Your honor," Stein asserted. "I object to what the defendant is doing."

"I object too,' said the judge. "Mr. Samson, you stop these tactics or I'll have you locked up! You leave the jurors out of this."

"But, your honor, Elliott Mess—"

The judge interrupted, "That will be all, Mr. Samson!"

Samson turned back to the jury to finish his closing. "Do you want to live in a country where IRS agents can scare jurors into pretending they have to go to the bathroom when they really wanted to report jury tampering?" He walked slowly back to his seat and sank into it.

Dubious Philosophical Musings

Part IV
The Constitution

"The most cogent reason for restricting the interference of government is the great evil of adding unnecessarily to its power."
—John Stuart Mill

"Only government can take perfectly good paper, cover it with perfectly good ink, and make the combination worthless."
—Milton Friedman

Most Americans regard the Constitution with reverence. We tend to assume that after the Constitutional Convention of 1787, everyone recognized how wonderful it was and we were ready to start our new country. But in fact there was vehement opposition to the Constitution. Americans had fought a revolutionary war against a government with too much power, and many feared the Constitution would create a new centralized federal government which also had too much power. It was in doubt whether the proposed Constitution would be ratified.

Enter James Madison, Alexander Hamilton, and John Jay. They wrote "The Federalist Papers," to reassure the citizenry that they had nothing to fear from the Constitution because its grant of power to the federal government was limited. James Madison, the "father" of the Constitution, cautioned against allowing "the essential characteristics of the Government as composed of limited and enumerated powers to be destroyed." He said that the "powers delegated by the proposed Constitution to the federal government are few and defined..."

Some 48 years later, in 1835, Alexis de Tocqueville, in *Democracy in America*, observed that a defining feature of American society was the notable absence of government. The Founding Fathers' plan to maximize individual freedom by creating a government with limited powers had succeeded. For the first 125 years after its creation, the federal government remained small, constrained within the limits of power imposed by the Constitution. That began to change in the early 20th century. For the past 100 years the federal government has steadily expanded its size, scope, and power, creating the huge federal bureaucracy that we live under today.

The federal government of today exercises a huge array of powers not authorized by the Constitution. Through Fannie Mae, Freddie Mac, and the FHA, the government controls the real estate mortgage market, which gives it dominion over the residential real estate market. Through the Federal Reserve Bank, the SEC, FDIC, and other agencies, the government controls the monetary system, the banks, brokerage firms and securities industry. It owns the railroads, and regulates the airline industry, airports, public transportation, the energy, oil and gas industries, and nuclear power. The government now has a dominant position in the automotive industry. It controls the student loan business, the public airwaves, public broadcasting, and telecommunications. It spends billions of dollars to create new industries, like wind and solar, which would be unable to survive without government support. It spends billions more to pay farmers to grow corn to produce ethanol, which costs more than and is less efficient than gasoline. This policy produces shortages of corn for food, driving up the cost of food for everyone in the world. Although ethanol subsidies have been justified by politicians in the name of reducing so called greenhouse gases, environmentalists now concede that ethanol produces no environmental benefit. Yet the subsidies continue.

The government subsidizes agriculture, and oversees food safety and pharmaceuticals. Decades ago government took over medical care and insurance for the elderly (Medicare) and the poor (Medicaid), and through Obamacare, is now taking charge of medical care and insurance for everybody else. The federal government provides oversight and financial subsidies for public education, and through FEMA has taken charge of relief from natural disasters. It has created and controls a mandatory retirement system for all U.S. citizens (Social Security), and sets wage, safety, and labor standards for workers. It provides hundreds of billions of dollars in hand outs for food stamps, housing subsidies, disability payments, unemployment benefits, and welfare for the benefit of the poor. It even gives away free telephones. It gives hundreds of billions of dollars in bank bailouts, corporate takeovers, and loan guarantees for the benefit of the rich. The federal government tells us how fast we can drive on the freeways, and regulates what kind of light bulbs, shower heads, and toilets we can buy. It spies on our bank and credit card records, our library records, our phone logs, emails, social networks, and will soon be using thousands of drone aircraft, like the kind used for surveillance of terrorists in Afghanistan, to spy on American citizens right here in our own country.

Who could say today that the federal government fits within James Madison's description of a "government composed of limited and enumerated powers?" Is there any area of life over which the government has not extended its tentacles? The plan of limited government created by our Founding Fathers in Philadelphia in 1787 has been overthrown. The limited government has been replaced by a government of unlimited powers, unbounded by Constitutional restraint.

There's a connection between these "musings" and our story. Sam Samson didn't like the government. Samson's dislike for government wasn't philosophical; it was personal. He saw business as a monopoly game, and the money was the way you keep score. But the government was constantly interrupting the game, picking up the board, randomly tossing the pieces around, and otherwise being obnoxious. He hated the government, not because of some libertarian theory of political philosophy. He just didn't like being told what to do by annoying, petty, power-hungry government bureaucrats who weren't as smart as he was.

Chapter 22

Exodus

The Old Testament: The Death of Samson

Now the rulers of the Philistines assembled …to celebrate, saying, "Our god has delivered Samson, our enemy, into our hands."…. Then Samson prayed to the LORD, ' Sovereign LORD, remember me. Please, God, strengthen me just once more, and let me with one blow get revenge on the Philistines for my two eyes.' Then Samson reached toward the two central pillars on which the temple stood. Bracing himself against them, his right hand on the one and his left hand on the other, Samson said, 'Let me die with the Philistines!' Then he pushed with all his might, and down came the temple on the rulers and all the people in it."
—Judges 16

"They sentenced me to twenty years of boredom, for trying to change the system from within. I'm coming now, I'm coming to reward them. First we take Manhattan – then we take Berlin."
—Leonard Cohen

Under the Plan for Universal Compliance, the IRS had created a new public relations division charged with seeing that tax evasion prosecutions received maximum publicity.

Publicizing the prosecution of ordinary citizens was designed to raise the public intimidation quotient and thereby increase compliance with the code. Samson's trial had received more news coverage than routine tax evasion trials of the past. When the jurors returned from deliberation, the gallery was half full, including some reporters. The judge had not yet entered the courtroom, and there was a buzz of background noise as everyone awaited the verdict. Stein turned around in his seat and was talking to Mess, seated behind him on the other side of the railing. Delilah sat in the back next to Buddha.

Pete and Isaac were out in the hallway. They walked down the hall past two guards who stood outside the courtroom door.

The bailiff said, "All rise," as the judge entered the courtroom. The judge said to be seated, then asked if the Jury had reached a verdict. The jurors looked nervously at Elliott Mess. The jury foreman stood to deliver the verdict. Samson sat back in his seat with his hands behind his head, as if he didn't have a care in the world. "Your honor," the foreman said, "we reluctantly find the defendant guilty on all counts of income tax evasion, failing to file tax returns, and assaulting a federal official's fist with his face."

Samson leaped to his feet. "Your honor, I move for a mistrial. Elliott Mess threatened to audit the jurors, and go after family members."

"Come now, Mr. Samson. You've been indulging in outrageous antics throughout this trial. And now this? We're all aware of Agent Ness's impeccable reputation for integrity from his work with 'The Untouchables.'"

"'The Untouchables?' But, your honor, that's a different guy!"

"Enough already!" she said, visibly irritated. "The verdict is upheld." She slammed her gavel. Samson sat down, slouching, apparently resigned to his fate. Two uniformed guards came from the back and stood behind Samson.

"The defendant will be held in custody and taken to the federal penitentiary in Lompoc, California, pending sentencing," the judge said. Samson turned suddenly as if looking around for an escape route, but before he could act, the guards grabbed hold of him from behind, and handcuffed him. In the back of the courtroom Elliott Mess handed a check to Buddha and a check and set of car keys to Samson's corvette to Delilah, again speaking to her inaudibly. She giggled. Buddha and Delilah left together, with Samson eyeing them, as the guards escorted him out of the courtroom.

• • •

Delilah and Buddha left the courthouse and got into Samson's Corvette, which was parked in front and sped off. Delilah had been given the sports car as a bonus for the excellent work she'd done on the case. Meanwhile, the guards escorted Samson out to a prisoner transport van parked in front of the courthouse, placed him in the back seat, and drove off.

As one of the guards drove the van down the road, the other got into the back seat and laughing, removed Samson's handcuffs. The "guard" was Isaac. The other "guard," Pete, was driving. After taking off the handcuffs Isaac returned to the front passenger seat. Samson, seated in the rear, rubbed his wrists and stretched his arms. "Where'd you guys get the guard uniforms?" he asked.

"The courthouse," Pete said.

"What happened to the real guards?" Samson asked.

Isaac and Pete looked at each other, then at Samson, and shrugged their shoulders. "I guess they got tied up," Isaac said, which was correct. The two real guards were at that moment lying in a small office in the courthouse, stripped to their underwear, gagged, and literally "tied up."

As they were driving down the highway, there was static and random talk coming over the police radio system, which they were ignoring. But when a female dispatcher's voice kept demanding, "PTV 16, respond immediately! Urgent! Urgent! Respond immediately!" it dawned on them that they were PTV (prisoner transport van) 16.

Isaac picked up the microphone. "This is PTV sixteen."

"Where the hell have you been?" asked the dispatcher. "Our GPS tracking shows you eight miles off course and headed in the wrong direction."

"Oh, that," said Isaac. "See, um, we ran into a situation, but don't worry. We're on our way."

Pete ripped the GPS device off the dashboard and opened the passenger side window. He handed the device to Isaac and signaled to him. Isaac threw it out the window. They happened to be on a bridge, and the GPS sailed over the rails into the river below.

"Negative," responded the dispatcher. "You are not on your way. You are behind schedule and headed in the wrong direction."

"Oh," Isaac said. "Don't worry about that. See my partner here wanted to stop at Starbucks and there was none on the way. That's all."

"You went off course to stop at a Starbucks?" the dispatcher asked incredulously.

"Yeah, y'know, just for a few minutes."

"While transporting a prisoner?"

"Um…" Isaac stammered.

"Stopping for food with a prisoner on board violates Section 1204 (b) of the federal prisoner transport code."

"No, you're incorrect about that. The code only prohibits entering a dining facility," Isaac improvised. "There's no explicit prohibition against ordering takeout at the window."

"Negative!" the dispatcher asserted. "The precedents are well established. Section 1204 (b) is subject to interpretation in the light of catch twenty-three."

Samson went slightly ballistic. "I hate that fucking 'catch twenty-three'!" he said.

"What?" said the dispatcher.

"Oh, that's nothing," said Isaac. "That was just the prisoner."

"The prisoner? What the—"

"He was expressing his opinion about catch twenty-three."

"Look, the prisoner is not permitted to express his opinion about catch twenty-three. That's a violation of Section 1625 (f). This is the third irregular incident you guys have been involved in this year. This is going to be subject to an administrative review. And in the meantime, you're completely off the GPS grid now. I'm turning in a code yellow alert."

"No, no, no, don't do that," Isaac pleaded. "We're on our way to the prison. Everything's under control—"

"Yeah, that's what you told me the other night too, Stanley, before you— Never mind!" Isaac wondered who Stanley was and what he had done.

"Look, baby" he said, improvising again, "I meant to apologize about the other night." Isaac was nothing if not fast on his feet.

"Very smooth," Samson whispered.

"What the hell are you talking about?" the dispatcher asked.

"Okay, maybe not that smooth," Samson said.

"I'm turning in a code yellow," the dispatcher continued. "Over and out!"

"Hello? Hello?" Isaac said. "Anybody there? Hello? Damn!" He hung up the microphone. "I think we gotta problem."

"Yeah, well, we gotta lotta problems, but there's not much we can do about it. Did Buddha give you the codes?" Samson asked.

Isaac fumbled around in his pockets looking for something. He found a crumpled piece of paper and looked at it, then held it tight in his hand as if not wanting to give it up. "Look, Sam," he said, "we don't have time to stop. They're gonna figure out what happened. And that bitch already turned in a code yellow. We gotta get away."

"No, Isaac, we gotta do it," Samson insisted.

"But we'll get caught. Buddha already got the money. There's nothing in it for you. Let's get the hell outta here. You heard her. She's turning in a code yellow."

"What's a code yellow?" Samson asked.

"I don't know."

"So you're going into a panic over a code yellow, and you don't even know what a code yellow is?'

"I know it's bad."

"I don't give a damn. I promised I'd do it so I'm gonna do it." Samson picked up a cell phone and dialed.

The receptionist answered, "Internal Revenue Service, regional office."

Samson, affecting a Middle Eastern accent, said, "This is Kahlid Sheik Mohammed's brother, Mohammed Mohammed.

You have ten minutes to clear the building before it blows up," and hung up. Pete accelerated and turned on the transport van's flashing lights, cars in front of them clearing out of their way as they raced down the freeway.

Isaac knew Samson was bullheaded, and that once he'd made up his mind there was no talking him out of it. Isaac was willing to take a risk to help his friend, but there are limits. If they took the time to stop at the IRS building and did what Samson wanted to do, there was almost no chance of escape and they'd all end up in the penitentiary. There was only one way to prevent Samson from launching this insane attack. Isaac opened the window.

Samson saw what Isaac had in mind. Before he could throw the codes out the window, Samson lunged forward, and grabbed Isaac around the throat. Isaac hit Samson's forearms with an upward thrust of his arm, releasing Samson's chokehold on his throat, but dropping the codes in the process. Samson came over the top of the seat, and as they wrestled, he spotted the piece of paper between the seats. He reached down to grab it, as Isaac gave him a rabbit punch to the back of the neck. With the code in his hand, he lunged back over the seat, Isaac still trying to wrestle with him. But as he dove over, he accidentally kicked Pete's arms just as Pete was turning on the siren. The van was just pulling into its destination, the IRS regional office building, but the kick caused Pete to lose his grip on the steering wheel. The van crashed into the guard tower in front of the building, the siren still blaring.

"I bail your sorry ass outta jail! I put you up at my place when you got nowhere else to go, bro! I risk getting my own ass thrown in jail to save your butt! And this is how you pay me back?" Isaac said.

"Don't worry, I'll pay you back," Samson responded.

"Okay, fine, you obviously feel strongly; we'll do it your way. And see how it works out."

As the three men got out of the van, they saw people running out of the building in a panic. Samson noticed the regional supervisor running out the front door. He quickly bent down facing the van, to tie his shoe, so the supervisor wouldn't see him. Isaac carried a black briefcase, Pete a tool box. A security guard, stunned by the impact of the van crashing into his guard house, came out. Seeing Pete, Isaac, and Samson turning toward the building he held up his hand for them to stop. "You can't go in there," he said. "There's been another bomb threat."

"*Another* bomb threat?" Samson asked.

"Yeah, we get 'em all the time."

"We're the bomb squad," Samson said.

The security guard eyed Isaac's and Pete's uniforms, and looked back over at the transport van, which looked official enough to pass muster as a bomb squad vehicle. However, he was suspicious because it was unorthodox for the bomb squad vehicle to crash into the guard house.

"You guys sure got here fast," the guard said.

"Yeah, well, we were in the neighborhood," Isaac answered, "y'know, disabling a bomb at EPA headquarters."

Samson, Isaac, and Pete ran in the front entrance. The building was deserted. Pete and Isaac stood guard while Samson worked at Elliott Mess's computer, looking repeatedly back and forth at the codes and the monitor. A police siren whined in the background, getting closer as Samson worked as quickly as possible. When he finished, he looked at Isaac and Pete and nodded. They rushed out of the building as the siren reached a crescendo.

Samson, Pete, and Isaac spotted the security guard as they went out and suddenly slowed down to a walk, trying to appear calm, as if everything was normal, despite the sirens.

"Did you find the bomb?" the guard asked.

"We found it," Isaac said.

"Well did you dismantle it?" asked the guard.

"Not yet," Pete said.

"Where you going?" the guard persisted.

Two police cars raced up the street coming into view in front. "It's lunch time. Union rules. We get a one-hour break," Isaac said, looking at the police cars, then at his watch. One police car practically crashed into the rear of the other as they came to a screeching stop. An official-looking van with a flashing red light on its roof pulled up next to them and double parked in the street. Samson looked at his watch. The doors to the police cars flew open. Isaac, Pete, and Samson tried to avoid giving the impression that they were in a hurry to leave as they started backing away from the guard toward the prisoner transport van, which had a broken headlight from the earlier crash into the guard house.

"But what about the bomb?" the guard shouted.

"Don't like to work on an empty stomach," Pete said

"Don't worry. We'll be back after lunch," Samson said. The guard looked at them incredulously as they piled into the van in a mad dash, and drove off, pulling away from the curb even before the door of the van was closed. As they raced off among the police cars, Samson said, "I think we're in trouble."

"What you mean 'we,' white man?" Pete said.

"You took that line from Tonto," Samson said.

"No, Tonto never said that," Pete said.

"He's right," Isaac added. "It wasn't actually Tonto. It was a *Mad* magazine spoof of Tonto."

As they pulled out, the police rushed over to the guard. Three officers in uniform jumped out of the other van holding black suitcases and also ran up to the guard. "We're the bomb squad," one of the officers said. "Is the building clear?"

Samson, Isaac, and Pete sped off in the van trying to get away before the police figured out what had happened. "Photo radar," Isaac shouted. "Slow down!" Pete slowed down, as they approached a photo radar device at an intersection. Pete took out his pistol, reached out the window in front of the windshield with his left hand, and shot the photo radar device, smashing the glass. The photo radar device made a horrible sound, like a distressed robot being demolished in a sci-fi film. Isaac patted Pete on the shoulder. "Good shot, now you can speed up," he said.

"You guys," Samson said, "just hijacked two federal court security guards, helped a convicted felon escape, stole a government vehicle, threatened to blow up a federal office building, and hacked into the IRS computer system. And you're worried about getting a speeding ticket?"

"Photo radar goes into a government database," Pete said.

"Yeah," Isaac said. "They're watching us."

Dubious Philosophical Musings

Part V

Distribution of Wealth

*"The inherent vice of capitalism
is the unequal sharing of blessings;
the inherent virtue of socialism
is the equal sharing of miseries."*
—Winston Churchill

*"The cripple that you feed and clothe
is neither starved nor cold."*
—Leonard Cohen

Laissez-faire capitalism is unpopular because it produces vast inequality in material wealth, power, and social status. This hurts people's feelings. Capitalism produces winners and losers. And like the kids on the losing Little League team, some long-term losers suffer from low self-esteem. I don't say this to minimize the problem. It's a real issue and it explains the existence of the Democratic Party in the United States and the socialist parties in the social democracies of Europe. These feelings of inadequacy, based on wealth inequality, are at the heart of the social democratic welfare state movement that drives politics in every democratic country.

The core issue in modern democracies is how to divide up the pie. Would you like to live in a society that has a huge pie that is divided unevenly, where some people have huge pieces of pie and others tiny pieces? Or a society with a small pie where everyone gets an equally small piece? Citizens of democracies try in vain to avoid this dilemma. They think they can find some way to produce a huge pie and still divide it equally. But this is impossible. Any policy that reduces the unequal distribution of the pie shrinks the pie. And the more even the distribution of wealth, the smaller the pie and the smaller the piece everybody gets.

The state can't redistribute wealth without damaging the incentives that create wealth. Those who have wealth don't give it to the government voluntarily. The government can only collect taxes to redistribute wealth with the threat of force. But the higher those who create wealth are taxed the less wealth they create. Raising tax rates creates disincentives for those who produce wealth. The higher the tax rates, the less wealth is produced. Higher tax rates shrink the pie. In political economics this is axiomatic, and those who deny it are in denial.

The welfare state also creates perverse incentives for those on the bottom side of the economic divide. The more largesse the poor receive from the welfare state, the less incentive they have to get off the dole and transform themselves into producers. If there are fewer producers there is less wealth to go around. The welfare state creates a class of chronic dependents. Welfare dependency is transmitted from generation to generation. Feeding at the public trough debilitates and degrades the poor, deterring them from developing the skills they need to make it in the market place. Redistributing wealth comes at a cost, making the entire society poorer and causing the most damage to those it's supposed to help.

In a pure democracy, where the guiding principle is "majority rules," there is little to prevent the poorest 51 percent from voting to appropriate to themselves the wealth of the richest 49 percent. Those who use the power of the state under the guise of majority rule to enrich themselves in this manner don't regard it as theft; they do it in the name of lofty-sounding principles such as equality, fairness, and social justice.

But it's difficult for the poorest 51 percent to forcibly collect money from the richest 49 percent. Therefore the advocates of redistribution use percentages more heavily skewed to tip the balance of power in their favor. We've all heard the pleas of the so called 99 percent to seize the wealth of the top 1 percent. Of course this isn't called "seizing wealth;" it is called something more euphonious like "making the rich pay their fair share." Somehow "fair share" is universally understood to mean "more." We never hear the argument that the rich should pay their "fair share" by paying *lower* taxes. The argument that, for the sake of fairness, tax rates on the rich should be lowered would make more sense since tax rates on the rich are substantially higher than rates on average income folks. The masses think it's fair that someone else should pay higher taxes, but they themselves shouldn't. People's sense of what's "fair" generally coincides with their own self-interest.

If there were really a struggle between the 99 percent and the 1 percent, the 1 percent would be in deep shit. When the 99 percent turn against the 1 percent it's the stuff of violent revolution, in which case the 1 percent don't fare that well. Think: French Revolution, Russian Revolution. The real divide in our democratic republic is more like 60 percent versus 40 percent. Opinion polls show that 60 percent think taxes should be raised on the rich. The media is astonished that the majority of voters favor raising someone else's taxes but not their own.

The rich are a persecuted minority. There is general consensus that it's morally justifiable to use the power of the state to take their money. The rich find little sympathy for the argument that they have constitutional rights, that ought to be protected against the ravages of majoritarian greed.

To you levelers, to you egalitarians, you know who you are. If you told pollsters you want to raise taxes on the rich, you are a leveler. If you voted for Obama because you wanted to make the rich pay their "fair share," you are a leveler. For you levelers, I've got a great deal for you. Here's my offer: You give up one half your wealth. The size of your house is cut in half. You trade in your car for an old one that's worth half as much. You give up your cell phone and eating in restaurants. Your material lifestyle is cut in half. What do you get in return for giving up half of everything you have? You get to see Bill Gates living next door to you on one side, and Warren Buffett on the other side, and they're both just as poor as you. Isn't that great? No more envy. No more sleepless nights worrying about how much richer your neighbor is than you.

Do you take the deal? Are you willing to give up half of your wealth for the joy of living in an egalitarian society where no one is richer than you? If you answer "yes," it means you hate capitalism, hate inequality, that you are a believer in the politics of envy and class warfare, and that you are pathetically envious and self-loathing. As long as you feel this way, you'll never be successful or happy.

Perhaps you'll respond that this is a reductio ad absurdum argument. No one, you'll say, really wants to bring Gates and

Buffett down so badly they're willing to impoverish themselves to do so. But in practice, when the middle class use the ballot box to penalize the rich, they get hoisted by their own petard, and make themselves poorer as well. Personally, I have no interest in raising taxes on the super rich. I'd rather help the poor by letting Gates and Buffett keep their money to invest, and hire poor people so they won't be poor anymore.

It's simplistic to think you can solve the problem of poverty by having government bureaucrats take money from some people and hand it out to others. Trillions of dollars have been spent on the "War on Poverty" since it was created in the 1960s and it's had no effect in reducing poverty. When you give poor people money, it actually perpetuates poverty. See, poverty isn't a lack of money. Poverty is ignorance. And giving poor people free money makes them *more* ignorant, dependent, and ultimately, poorer. Free handouts subsidize and promulgate the bad habits and poor choices that lead to poverty.

The rich don't have enough money to fund the huge nanny state bureaucracy. So when they've bled the rich as much as feasible, the redistributionists must turn their fire against the middle class as well. When the political class's addiction to excessive government spending spins out of control, the government runs out of middle-class money also. Then it's off to the bond markets, and eventually, as the national debt mushrooms out of control, to the printing presses. Of course these days they don't even need printing presses. The Federal Reserve magically creates money with digital entries in government computers and hands it out like candy at Halloween to favored banks and Wall Street firms to do God knows what with. Central bankers say this policy of creating money out of thin air, which they call "quantitative easing," and giving it to their crony capitalist banker buddies is good for the economy. It's hard to know whether these financial megalomaniacs actually believe such palpable poppycock. But it's not hard to understand why the rest of us, who aren't blessed with this government largesse for the rich, are skeptical of its benefits.

The elitist ruling class, which governs us from that cesspool of corruption and decadence in Washington, cloaks its policies in the language of altruism and compassion. These effete statists believe that we peasants out in the hinterlands are incompetent to manage our lives without help from the enormous bureaucracy they've erected to run this country, a bureaucracy which, in reality, primarily benefits the politicians who created it, and public officials who run it.

Critics will say I'm engaging in a tirade against the poor. But I'm not. It's a tirade against demagogue politicians who use the poor as pawns and props, who accumulate power by using other people's money to buy votes. If you buy into the notion that government should decide how wealth should be allocated, in the name of helping the needy, what makes you think that government will limit its handouts only to the needy? The political class inexorably expands the definition of "needy" until it includes everybody. The more money politicians hand out, the more power they accrue for themselves. So they decide we're *all* needy. We *all* need the government to manage our retirement. We *all* need the government to oversee our healthcare.

The same politicians who vote for welfare state benefits for the poor are equally generous with the middle class and the rich. They vote for trillion dollar "tarp" bailouts for banks, trillion dollar "stimulus" packages to create "shovel ready" jobs that aren't "shovel ready" and never materialize. They give farm subsidies to millionaire farmers, business subsidies to crooked businessmen who make political contributions, and a variety of handouts to thousands of highly profitable "nonprofits" with dubious agendas. Naturally those who receive these trillions of dollars of public largesse generously pay back the politicians who give them our money by helping them get re-elected, so they can give them even more of our money.

Do you think it's possible to clean up this Aegean Stable of corruption while the government is handing out $3.8 trillion a year? The only way to clean up this stinking mess is for the government to stop giving away money. But don't hold your breath. This ain't gonna happen until Washington's fiscal profligacy, camouflaged by the Fed's easy money, debases our currency to the point of no return. Then the currency will collapse, our financial system will collapse, and the political storm that follows will, as Dylan put it, "shake your windows and rattle your walls."

Chapter 23
The Empire Strikes Back

*"If you get into an argument with a fool,
a passerby won't know which one is the fool."*
—Chinese proverb

*"The man in the trench coat, badge out, laid off…
wants to get paid off… Look out kid, it's something you did,
God knows when but you're doing it again."*
—Bob Dylan

The van with Pete, Isaac, and Samson raced into the airport, a small rural facility, normally very quiet. It had some small one- and two-engine airplanes, and a couple of helicopters. The parking lot merged with the grass and modest tarmac. Buddha was already there, leaning against Samson's Corvette, working on his smart phone. Delilah exited the terminal building holding a set of keys and a document. She walked quickly toward the Corvette.

The van raced into the parking lot and parked behind the Corvette. Pete, Isaac, and Samson jumped out. Pete shook Buddha's hand, as Delilah came up and embraced him. Then Samson noticed something peculiar: a crowd of reporters and a TV news camera crew gathered by the terminal. When they spotted Samson and his gang they dashed toward them. Samson gestured at the reporters and cameras. "What's all this?" he asked Delilah.

"I thought you'd like some publicity," she explained.

"Have you lost your mind?"

"Look, Sam. You need the press on your side. Otherwise, what kind of spin do you think the IRS'll give this?"

Reporters crowded around and shoved microphones in Samson's face, asking him a bunch of questions all at once. Samson held up his hand for them to quiet down. The TV cameras were rolling.

Reporter # 1 asked, "Mr. Samson, is it true the IRS rigged your trial?"

"Look, I don't want to snivel," Samson said. "They just followed standard procedures."

"You mean they stole your money, beat you up, and threatened to audit the jurors to get a guilty verdict?" the reporter asked.

"Yeah, just the usual stuff." Samson was surprised at how well informed the reporter was.

"Where are you headed?" reporter #2 asked.

"As far away as possible. I'll send you a postcard."

"Mr. Samson—" reporter #3 began.

But Samson broke away and began backing slowly toward the plane, still facing the reporters, Delilah at his side. Isaac and Pete were already boarding the plane. Buddha was making a video recording of everything.

"Sorry to be rude," Samson interrupted, "but I'm kind of in a hurry. But I want you to know. I have a surprise for the American people. You'll find out soon what I'm talking about. And that's what I want to be remembered for when I die, which could be any moment."

Samson abruptly turned and ran toward the plane, holding hands with Delilah running by his side. In the near-distance, sirens approached, getting louder. Samson and Delilah quickly boarded the plane, waving goodbye to the reporters who moved as a flock toward the plane.

. . .

Samson sat in the pilot seat of the six-seater, Delilah beside him, and started fiddling with the controls of the unfamiliar plane. The other three men sat down and put on their seatbelts. Samson didn't have time to do the usual safety checks, but he got the plane started and the engine roaring as two police cars, sirens blaring, raced into the airport. The police officers jumped out of their cars. They saw the plane starting down the runway and pulled their guns. Elliott Mess and his younger sidekick agent drove up in another car. They jumped out and pulled their guns too. As the plane taxied down the runway, the reporters pulled back to get out of the line of fire, but the TV cameras kept rolling. The police and IRS agents fired at the plane, as it picked up speed. Ducking bullets, everyone on board waved good-bye out the windows, which was perceived as a friendly goodbye gesture by reporters and a taunt by the IRS agents. Bullets grazed the outside of the plane, and as the plane lifted off a bullet shot out one tire.

"Landing with a blown tire may be a bit of a challenge," Samson said. But at least the plane was getting out of firing range. Everyone on board sat back and breathed easier as the plane gained altitude.

"Are you sure you wanna escape, Sam?" Delilah asked, somewhat belatedly.

"My tribe has a saying," Pete said. "When the going gets tough, the tough take a vacation."

"What tribe do you belong to, Pete?" Delilah asked.

"I'm Jewish," Pete said. Everybody looked at Pete funny.

"Hey, Pete," Isaac said, "did you really fight Hulk Hogan?"

"Twice," Pete answered.

"How'd you do against him?"

"I lost."

"How come you lost, Pete?" Buddha asked.

"It was fixed."

"Wait a minute," Isaac said. "You think if it wasn't fixed, you coulda beat Hulk Hogan?"

"Probably not."

"How did you get the plane, Delilah?" Samson asked.

"It had a tax lien on it. Elliott Mess signed the release order."

"Mess signed the release order?" Samson asked incredulously. "How'd you get him to sign the order?"

"He trusts me."

"Elliott Mess trusts you?"

"Why shouldn't he?"

One reason Samson found Delilah so attractive was that she could give such an answer and sincerely mean it. Although Delilah had many positive character traits, trustworthiness didn't stand out as an obvious one. She was, after all, a professional deceiver and it seemed absurd that anyone with half a brain would trust her, least of all Elliott Mess. The fact that she really believed that Mess trusted her was an authentic expression of her innocence. Samson found the paradoxes of her character irresistible, that she could be such a dangerous, devious femme fatal' and seductress, yet still emanate this quality of innocence. It reminded him of Marilyn Monroe. He also liked her hot body.

...

It appeared to Isaac that they were out of danger and on their way, so he thought this would be a good time to talk to Samson about a business idea he'd been pondering. "Sam, I gotta talk to you," he said.

"What is it?"

"I got a great idea how we can make money."

"Hey, Isaac," Samson responded, "this really isn't a good time. See that plane behind us?"

Isaac looked behind them. Following close on was an old fighter plane with gun turrets. "I think they're after us," Samson continued.

"Man, you think everyone's after you."

"Everyone *is* after me." As he spoke, a warning shot from the fighter plane passed next to them. Samson looked over at Isaac and shrugged his shoulders. "See?" he said.

But Isaac didn't regard the fact that they were being shot at as proof that someone was after them, and he continued to argue the point. "You're just paranoid," he said.

"Anyone who isn't paranoid isn't in touch with reality," Pete said. He took his pistol out of his holster and opened a window wide enough to stick the gun out. He started shooting in the direction of the fighter plane, but wildly and with considerable difficulty because of the wind force.

"What's the opposite of paranoid?" Samson asked.

"What are you talking about?" said Isaac.

"Well, paranoia is when you think people are out to get you, when they aren't. How about if you think no one is out to get you, when they really are? That's the opposite of paranoia. There oughta be a word for it. 'Cause that's what you are, Isaac. How about 'oblivious'?"

A shot from the fighter plane, which was clearly the IRS in hot pursuit, burst through the cockpit window, cutting Samson's cigar in half, before blowing out the adjacent window. Samson took the broken cigar out of his mouth and looked at it. "I hate that!" he said.

"About my idea—" Isaac persisted.

"I'm kinda busy right now," Samson interrupted, trying with little success to take evasive action.

"Man, you're always busy. Good managers make time to listen to employees' ideas."

"Al right. What is it?" As they spoke, Samson kept trying to maneuver the plane, as the gunfire continued. One of Pete's bullets happened to graze the IRS plane's windshield. Realizing that they were being fired on, the IRS plane dropped back a bit temporarily.

"Okay, I just want to say one word to you," Isaac said.

"Plastic?"

"Plastic? Huh? No. Condoms.

"Condoms."

"Yeah."

"Uh-huh."

"We can make a fortune," Isaac continued, "selling condoms."

"Yeah, that's great."

"You market them according to size: large, extra-large, huge, and afro."

"What about small?" Samson asked.

"Nobody's gonna buy 'small.'"

The IRS plane's fire resumed, occasionally grazing the plane and causing minor damage. Samson's efforts at evasive action didn't help much against the larger, faster IRS plane.

"That's a great idea. I'll give it some thought later today, if I'm still alive," Samson said.

"But, you know," he continued, "What's the deal with having a size called 'afro.' 'Afro' isn't really a size, is it? Isn't it more like a hair style?"

"No, man," Isaac said. "It's a hair style when you're talking about hair. But when you're talking about condoms, it's a size. You know, it means, like, the condom is very large."

"Well, I think that's a problem in terms of marketing," Samson rejoined. "I think you're perpetuating racial stereotyping there. I mean calling the largest size 'afro' is racist."

"No, that's not possible. How could it be racist?"

"Come on," Samson said. "Promulgating that old myth about afro size is definitely racist."

"How can it be racist, when it's coming from an African American?" Isaac rejoined.

"An African American, huh? Is that what you are?"

"Yeah, duh! What'd you think I am?"

"So if you're an African American, what am I?"

"You're a white guy."

"No, if you're an African American, I'm a European American,"

"No, dude, that's not how it works. I'm African American and you're white."

"No, if I'm white, then you're black."

"No, man, see *that's* racist."

"What's racist about it?"

"Calling me black. That's racist."

"Okay, so me calling you black is racist, but for you to call the large size condom 'afro,' that isn't racist?"

"No, how could it be racist, coming from an African American?"

"Okay, so let me get this straight. You're saying that nothing a black says can ever be racist?"

"Right, of course not. Because black people can't be racist. Only white people can be racist."

"I don't understand that."

"Because we're an oppressed minority. You're a privileged majority, see?"

"No, I don't see."

"Because my ancestors were brought here on slave boats, and forced into slavery, and oppressed and lynched by your ancestors for hundreds of years."

"I got news for you, pal," Samson argued. "My ancestors never oppressed your ancestors. My ancestors never lynched your ancestors. When your ancestors were being oppressed and lynched, my ancestors were being slaughtered in pogroms. But you don't hear me demanding that they have special condom sizes for Jews!"

"It doesn't have to be your direct ancestors. People who looked like you oppressed people who looked like me."

"Do you have a twin brother?"

"No."

"Well, then *nobody* looks like you. And I don't have a twin brother, so nobody looks like me either. Except maybe Tom Cruise. So do you think Tom Cruise oppressed your ancestors?"

"What? You think you look like Tom Cruise?"

"Yeah, only better looking."

"I got news for you, dude. You don't look anything like Tom Cruise. Hence your argument is irrelevant."

"That's illogical. Even if you're correct that I don't look like Tom Cruise, that doesn't make my argument irrelevant."

"Yeah it does. Because the premise of your argument is that you look like Tom Cruise. So if your premise is false, your entire argument is false."

"No. That's a nonsequitur. My looking like Tom Cruise isn't the premise of my argument. It's peripheral. It's your argument that's based on a false premise—that *my* ancestors oppressed *your* ancestors."

"No, you said you look like Tom Cruise, but frankly, you ain't no Tom Cruise. Therefore, your entire line of logic fails."

"You're missing the point."

"No, *you're* missing the point. The point is that you white folk oppressed us black folk for centuries. So if we hate you, it's not racism; it's justified. But we never did anything to *you*. So if you hate *us*, it's racism."

"Look, man, I appreciate that you risked your neck to keep me out of prison—"

"Yeah, I'm starting to think that was a mistake," Isaac interrupted, as a shell hit one of the engines and the propeller started sputtering.

"Jesus, would you guys shut up, already?" Delilah interjected. "I know you wanna do your part to set race relations back fifty years, but could you maybe continue this debate later, y'know, like when they stop shooting at us?"

As she spoke, the gas tank got hit by shrapnel, and burst into flames. The plane headed into a precipitous dive, smoke pouring out the back.

"God, those guys are jerks," Isaac said.

The IRS plane stayed on their tail as the plane headed down. Samson tried pulling it out, but to no avail. The engine caught fire. The burning plane headed toward the ground, spinning out of control, a crash clearly imminent. Delilah tightened her seat belt. "Next time let's take a commercial flight," she said.

"What?" Isaac objected. "And have to go though airport security?"

The plane crashed into the ground.

Dubious Philosophical Musings

Part VI

Inequality

"A man is likely to mind his own business when it is worth minding. When it is not, he takes his mind off his own meaningless affairs by minding other people's business."
—Eric Hoffer

"When a socialist harangued Andrew Carnegie about redistribution of wealth, Carnegie asked his secretary for two numbers—the world's population and the value of all his assets. He divided the latter by the former, then said to his secretary, 'Give this gentleman 16 cents. That is his share of my net worth.'"
—George Will

I don't presume to make the case that laissez faire capitalism allocates wealth fairly. I concede there's nothing fair about it. But the problem isn't capitalism. As John F. Kennedy put it, "life is unfair." And if life itself is unfair, then any effort to correct the perceived unfairness of the free market through public policy is doomed to failure. If you think capitalism is unfair, and your conscience is bothering you, then give away your own money. But don't imagine you can remedy the injustices of capitalism by using the power of the state to take other peoples' money and entrusting politicians and bureaucrats to hand it out. That's not fair either. So forget about fairness. There's no political solution to the "fairness" problem.

But if you don't heed my advice, and you're determined to try, despite the unintended consequences, to use the power of the state to redistribute wealth, first ask yourself this question: Is wealth the most important thing? What if you try to redistribute good looks, physical strength, athletic ability, or talent, or even (dare I say it?) intelligence? Is it fair that one person should be born big, strong, good looking, talented, and smart, while someone else is born weak, ugly, feeble, and stupid? If you think that's unfair, then take it up with God. That's just the way it is.

Would you rather be born into a wealthy family but have nothing going for you in inherited characteristics, or be born into a poor family and have Arnold Schwarzenegger's body and Mark Zuckerberg's brain? Obviously wealth is not the most significant inequality. So why do politicians and ideologues obsess about it? Because it's the only "injustice" these busybodies imagine they can do something about.

Arguably, inequality of wealth is not an evil which needs to be addressed by public policy at all. How does it harm you if Bill Gates has $50 billion? Why is that a problem? If equality becomes a goal of public policy it can only be achieved one way. It's not possible to achieve equality by making everybody equally rich; only by making everybody equally poor. Think: Soviet Union, Cuba, North Korea. Very egalitarian societies. How many limousine liberals would want to live there?

In prehistoric times humans had material equality. In hunter/gatherer societies what was the difference between the richest guy in the tribe and the poorest? Maybe the richest guy had an extra bear skin to give his wife, and he had a five-day supply of food instead of a three-day supply. Big deal.

The discovery of agriculture changed that. Bringing land under cultivation required a social system to assure the guy who was growing food that it was *his* land and *his* food, and no one could steal it from him. Unless you could "own" your own land, no one would grow food, only to see it stolen by others. This system of land ownership, based on civil society and law, produced inequalities in wealth as some people had more or better land than others. However, it also made agriculture possible, and provided a more varied, abundant, reliable, and higher quality supply of food, thereby diminishing the vicissitudes and hardships of the hunter/gatherer lifestyle. That's the tradeoff. To have higher material quality of life for the population overall it is necessary to also have greater inequality.

Thousands of years later the industrial revolution created far greater levels of wealth inequality. Capitalist manufacturers were able to amass huge fortunes by owning business entities that mass produced the products that everyone wanted. Again, the same tradeoff. The material comforts of modern life couldn't exist without the industrial system which inevitably generates huge inequalities of wealth. The question you should ask yourself, if you're troubled by wealth inequality, is whether you really want to lie awake at night in your comfortable bed, in your heated, insulated, modern home, worrying about how rich Warren Buffett is.

Chapter 24
Clear and Present Danger

"In the long run we're all dead."
—John Maynard Keynes

"To live beyond the law you must be honest."
—Bob Dylan

The site of the crash was a farm field in Missouri. The IRS plane flew over to check it out. Elliott Mess looked out the window at the wreckage below. They circled a couple of times, saw no one moving, then flew away. It was late afternoon, and as the daylight began to fade, the wreckage burned on the ground.

Then a foot kicked out through a broken window. The rest of Samson followed, dirty, disheveled, shaken, and a little bloody. Looking around, he realized the others were still in the plane. He reached back in and pulled out Delilah, who was a mess but hadn't broken any bones. She leaned on his arm as they limped away from the plane. He helped ease her onto a bank. She sat down, shell shocked, looking down at the wreckage.

Samson returned to the plane, took off his coat, and beat at the flames, as Isaac crawled out where the windshield had been. Pete carried Buddha out what was left of the tail and they started slowly toward where Delilah was sitting. Samson turned, limped away from the plane again, sat down next to Delilah, and lit a fresh cigar. Then what was left of the plane exploded. Samson and Delilah were numb and didn't react, as if they were expecting it. The explosion sent Pete, Isaac, and Buddha to the ground. They crawled over to join Samson and Delilah. They sat there on the bank, the five of them, covered in soot, unmoving, haplessly staring at the burning wreckage, exhausted, in shock, no one giving a thought what to do next.

Then, like an apparition out of the dense smoke, the tall, shrouded figure of a man silently appeared, walking towards them, the setting sun at his back. It was the farmer on whose land they were sitting. In unison they stared blankly at him, seemingly indifferent to the shotgun he had aimed at them, and to whatever catastrophe might occur next. The farmer stared back at them for a long moment, without moving.

"Was that the IRS?" he asked. There was a long pause.

"What?" Samson finally replied.

"That shot you down."

"What gives you that idea?"

"Oh, they shot down my son-in-law last year, back in Iowa."

"Why?"

"He's a tax protester. Are you a tax protester?"

"No, but I'm thinking about becoming one," Samson said.

"I'd advise against it. They don't have much tolerance for tax protesters."

"They're not real fond of me anyway."

"No, it doesn't look like they are. What have they got against you if you aren't a tax protester?"

"I'm a tax *cheater*."

"So that *was* the IRS shooting you down. Are you Sam Samson?"

"You *know* me?"

The farmer lowered his shotgun and grinned. "They've got your picture all over the TV. I guess you stuck it to those bastards."

Samson stood up. The farmer walked over and shook his hand.

"Say, would you have a vehicle you could sell us?" Samson asked. "I'll pay cash."

"Well, I got an old truck that still runs. I don't know how far it'll get. Where you headed?"

"We need to go about twelve-hundred miles."

The farmer reached into his pocket and pulled out a large ring of keys. He sorted through them, and handed the key to the truck to Samson, as the other members of the group pulled themselves up.

"You might make it," said the farmer. "I don't have a title; it's got a tax lien on it."

"It doesn't matter. We're kind of in a hurry. How much do you want?"

"Oh, hell. It's not worth much. Just take it. And good luck. A lotta folks are rooting for you."

Pete, Isaac, Buddha and Delilah were managing to stay up on their feet as they dusted themselves off. Along with Samson, they followed the farmer to his tool shed, where the truck was kept. It was old and beaten up, and covered with dirt and dust. With some difficulty Samson got the door opened and tried to start it, but the battery was dead. The farmer went to get his other pickup and jumper cables as Pete opened the hood. After a couple of tries they were able to get it jump started, and a plume of blue smoke blew out of the exhaust pipe. The farmer gave Samson a map and showed him where to go. The others piled in and the farmer watched them drive off.

...

Early the next morning a black car drove up to the farm house. Elliott Mess's sidekick agent rang the farmer's doorbell, and Mess knocked impatiently as they waited. The farmer, still in his pajamas, opened the door. Mess showed his badge. "Elliott Mess, special agent, Internal Revenue," he said.

"Look, I sent a check last month for the full amount," the farmer said. As he continued to look at Mess, he did a double take. "Say, didn't you used to be on 'The Untouchables?'"

"Different guy," said Mess. "Had any visitors recently?"

"Well, my daughter was here last spring, with her husband and my grandson. We don't do much entertaining."

"You didn't happen to notice a plane crash."

The farmer hesitated and stammered slightly. "P-Plane crash?"

Mess pointed toward the plane wreckage that was still burning in plain view a hundred yards from the house.

"I thought I heard something," the farmer said.

Mess grabbed the farmer, put him in a hammer lock, and shoved his head up against the door jam. "Listen, you ignorant, redneck, hayseed piece of dog shit, you tell me what I want to know right now or you will hereafter think of your life as falling into two distinct phases: before you met me, and after you met me. You've got five seconds to decide. One, two…"

The farmer grimaced in pain. He'd been a prisoner of war in Vietnam but that was a long time ago, and he didn't have the stomach for it any more. "I sold him my truck," he confessed. "I swear I don't know where he's going, but he said it's about twelve hundred miles. He had a woman with him, sexy as hell, and three men, one black, one Oriental, and a big Indian."

Mess released his grip. The farmer rubbed the back of his neck, but something had snapped and he was still in pain.

"Did the big guy look Jewish?" Mess asked.

"No, he looked like an Indian."

Mess and the other agent returned to the car and took out a map. They placed the map on the hood of the car, and Mess traced a path on it with his finger. "Twelve hundred miles. They were headed southeast. That means Florida. He must be headed for a tax haven. They'll get a boat and try to get out of the country."

Mess and the other agent didn't notice the farmer as they spoke. He felt bad about giving up the information so quickly. So while they were looking at the map, the farmer snuck over to the bushes near his driveway. He had an air rifle filled with BBs, a dozen of which he shot into their rear tire while they were looking at the map. They got back in their car, but as they started to roll they realized they had a flat. They got out, and Mess pounded the hood in frustration. Then they went to work changing the tire. The farmer waited in the bushes. When they were done, and got back into the car, he shot one more bb into the spare tire they'd just put on, enough to produce a slow leak. *That ought to slow down those bastards,* the farmer thought.

...

As Mess drove, his partner called in an APB for Sam Samson and his four traveling companions, believed to be headed toward Florida's east coast in an old pickup. A few minutes later they realized they had another flat and pulled over. This time they didn't have another spare. Mess began to suspect something. He went back in the trunk, pulled out the first flat tire, and shook it. He heard the BBs rolling around inside, and figured out what had happened. They got road service and got a new tire for the car; this cost them another two hours. Now he had a dilemma. Should he drive back to teach that SOB farmer a lesson or stay focused on tracking Samson?

Chapter 25
Irreconcilable Differences

"Mankind is now at an historic crossroads. One path leads to despair and utter hopelessness; the other path to total annihilation. Let us pray that we have the wisdom to choose the right path."
—Woody Allen

"When I am on a pedestal you did not raise me there. Your laws do not compel me to kneel grotesque and bare."
—Leonard Cohen

Samson knew the old pickup would never make it all the way to Florida. He also figured that Elliott Mess might pay a visit to the farmer and find out what they were driving. So when they got to a town they went to the first used car lot they saw and upgraded to an S.U.V. Samson paid cash and gave the dealer an extra $200 to avoid formalities like checking ID or notifying DMV who had purchased the car. They parked the old pickup in a supermarket parking lot and removed the license plates. To play it safe, Pete also filed off the vehicle identification numbers. They figured if they paid cash for their expenses, avoided video cameras, and kept a low profile, they might make it to Florida without being located by the government.

They made it without incident to a dock in a crowded Florida harbor. Samson had already wired a deposit on a boat he'd found online. The boat owner met them in the harbor. It was understood that it was a "no questions asked" cash deal. After quickly inspecting the boat, Samson handed the owner the balance of the money owed. The owner handed Samson the title and boat keys. They shook hands and the boat owner left. As they prepared the boat for departure, Isaac spotted Elliott Mess and his men at a distance at the other end of the dock and pointed them out to Samson.

Samson put on a big hat to conceal his identity and moved quickly to the controls and started the boat. Isaac, Buddha, and Delilah went below deck. Mess and his men boarded a coast guard ship. Samson steered his boat behind a large boat, blocking it from the view of the coast guard ship. Pete gestured for Samson to stop the boat. "Wait," he said. He took a huge knife out of a sheath attached to his belt and cut off a piece of hose coiled on the deck, and a section of rope. He put the knife back in the sheath, and stuck the section of hose into his belt. He looked through the boat's tool box and found a crowbar. He took off his shirt and dove into the water with the crowbar, rope, and hose.

Pete swam under the large boat to the back of the coast guard ship and silently surfaced. Still in the water, he felt his way along the hull until he found what he was looking for. Above him on the deck, two armed crewmen were smoking, laughing, suspecting nothing. Pete pried the fuel latch cap off with the crowbar, then dropped the crowbar, which sank to the sand below. Then he stuck the section of hose into the hole and sucked on it. Gasoline started leaking out the end of the siphon hose. Using his knife, Pete secured the hose in the hole with the rope and the chain from the gas cap. The crewmen heard something and fell silent. They looked over the side, and drew their revolvers. All they saw was water rushing into the spot Pete had just left as he dived back under the water.

...

"Dolphin," one crewman said.

As Pete was starting to siphon the gas below, Elliott Mess was in the command center of the ship, talking to someone at the Department of Homeland Security, trying to find out if any of the drones had located Samson yet, and arguing about what the drones would do when they did locate him. Mess's argument with a stubborn official at the Department of Homeland Security wasn't going well. Mess wanted the DHS to agree that if a drone located Samson it would take him out. But the DHS official said they couldn't do this because the law doesn't permit them to use drones to kill American citizens unless they are known terrorists. "Sam Samson *is* a known terrorist," Mess insisted. "He threatened to blow up IRS Regional Headquarters."

"Be that as it may," the DHS official replied, "he isn't a known terrorist because he's not on an agency list of known terrorists. Therefore, he can't be targeted for death." In addition, the DHS official pointed out, Samson was accompanied by several other people who were not known terrorists, including, he said, an undercover agent of the U.S. government, one Delilah something; he was unable to determine her last name. "It is against DHS policy," he explained, "to use drone aircraft to kill U.S. government agents. We'll use our drones and spy satellites to track this guy and help you find him. But I don't want to be hauled before Congress next time the wind shifts in Washington, so if you want to kill him, you're on your own, pal."

Mess argued that the prohibition against firing on U.S. citizens was subject to interpretation in light of catch 23. But the DHS official retorted that he *was* interpreting it in light of catch 23, and that was his interpretation, and that was that. Mess, exasperated, hung up, having lost several minutes, giving Samson time to get away undetected.

...

Pete emerged at Samson's boat, which was still hidden from view of the coast guard ship. Samson and Isaac pulled him on board. Then they quickly headed out, motoring north up the coast line so the coast guard ship wouldn't see them. When they got out of view of the harbor, they headed out toward freedom and the open seas.

They raced across the swells, Samson steering. Isaac was the first to see the coast guard ship come into view on the horizon.

Mess stood on the bridge, scanning the ocean with binoculars, until he located Samson's boat. The coast guard ship raced through the water, gradually closing the gap between the two vessels. The coast guard ship finally pulled within earshot, and aimed its high-powered weapons at Samson's boat. Mess spoke into an electric bull-horn. "Cease and heave to," he said.

Unfortunately, the sound quality was poor, and as he spoke, someone blew the ship's horn, so all that could be heard was the consonant "s" and the sound "oo."

"What did he say?" Samson asked.

"It sounded like 'screw you,'" Isaac said.

"Why would he say that?" Samson wondered.

But, as fate would have it, because of the gasoline leaking out, the coast guard ship engine started sputtering at that very moment. Samson saw that the ship's guns were directed at him, and figured his best chance to get away was to swing around behind the coast guard ship, the opposite side from where the guns were trained on him. As Samson's boat started to pull away and circle behind the incapacitated coast guard ship, Isaac and Delilah laughed, taunted, and waved goodbye to Mess. This was a bad idea.

"Open fire, men!" Mess shouted.

The coast guard ship sprayed Samson's boat with machine gun fire. Samson and crew hit the deck, as glass broke and everything came down around them. The engine raced, but no one steered as the boat arced around the coast guard ship in a semi-circle. The machine-gun fire continued to blast away, doing significant damage.

Delilah attached a white handkerchief to a stick and waved it up over the railing. Mess saw it. "Hold your fire, men!' he commanded. The gunfire stopped. Samson stayed down on the deck on his stomach, but worked his way back to the steering wheel. Delilah stood up cautiously. Across the water, she shouted, "Elliot, you stop shooting at us or I'm gonna file for divorce!"

Samson stuck his head up and stared at Delilah in astonishment, thunderstruck by the revelation that she was married to Mess. No wonder she didn't have a last name. Mess and his men opened fire again. Samson ducked down and Delilah hit the deck. Gunfire continued, bullets randomly striking the boat. But Samson, down on his knees and ducking, managed to steer the boat, which was now limping from engine damage, slowly away from the stalled coast guard ship. Delilah and the others remained on their stomachs on the deck.

"You're married to that tax-collecting maggot?" Samson asked.

"Yeah, didn't I tell you?"

"You neglected to mention it."

The machine gun fire continued.

"Actually, our marriage has been going through a rocky period," Delilah confessed.

"He didn't seem interested in reconciliation," Samson observed. "This kind of behavior is sometimes symptomatic of deeper problems in a relationship."

"What?"

"When your husband tries to kill you with a machine gun. Have you thought about counseling?"

"Yeah, maybe we should try counseling. We do seem to have some communication issues."

As the boat got further away from the Coast Guard ship, the machine-gun fire receded. Samson and the others cautiously stood up. Samson noticed that his cigar had again been destroyed by gunfire, this time leaving only a small smoldering stub. He took the cigar out of his mouth, looked at it, took one last drag, and then threw it overboard in irritation. "That's it!" he said. "I quit smoking!"

Unfortunately, the boat had gone off in the direction where the siphon leak had left the most gasoline on the surface of the water. The cigar landed in the gasoline which caught fire. The flame raced back along the path of the gasoline to its source. "Shit!" Mess said. The ship exploded. Mess and his crew jumped into the water. Samson's damaged boat limped off, its engine sputtering.

Dubious Philosophical Musings

Part VII

Taxes and Social Justice

"If you took all the money in the world and distributed it amongst all the people, within x amount of time – five years, three years, six months – the rich would be rich, and the poor would be poor. Why? Because some people know how to play Monopoly, and some people don't know how to play Monopoly."
—David Marshall

"Being elected to Congress is regarded as being sent on a looting raid for one's friends."
—George Will

It's a proven tenet of psychology, corroborated by hundreds of scientific studies, that behavior that is rewarded tends to be repeated, and behavior that is punished tends to be avoided. Despite this undisputed truism, American public policy perversely punishes productive behavior and rewards unproductive behavior. We reward indolence and failure by heavily subsidizing it. We punish work and success by heavily taxing it. As a result of these counterproductive policies, unemployment goes up, productivity goes down. Wealth is destroyed, poverty is expanded.

Then politicians react to the economic problems they've created with shock and dismay, and try to figure out whom to blame. They try to solve the problem by borrowing more money to create more government giveaway programs for the poor. Paying people not to work creates unemployment. Duh! The government gives out free money in the form of unemployment benefits, welfare, food stamps, housing subsidies, Medicaid, Social Security, disability, and free cell phones. Then they're amazed that the recipients of these freebies, who are able to get by on government largesse, can't find jobs. To paraphrase Samuel Johnson, nothing concentrates the attention as effectively as the knowledge that your unemployment benefits have run out. When your refrigerator is empty, it somehow becomes easier to find a job. (That's a basic principle of economics taught at the Wharton School). As long as government handouts to the poor continue, unemployment and poverty, and the social problems like drug abuse and broken families that accompany them, will go on forever.

So-called conservatives, who argue not that the welfare state should be entirely eliminated, but that welfare state spending should be "trimmed" so it only benefits the "truly needy," don't recognize that they've already lost the debate. They've accepted the fundamental premise of the welfare state—the pernicious notion that it's an appropriate function of government to provide financial subsistence for the citizenry.

Redistributing wealth requires the citizens to cede an enormous amount of power to the state. The tax collecting agency has to be granted extraordinary powers. People won't pay their taxes unless men with guns make them. If tax evasion is punished only with fines, taxpayers will soon figure out that the risk/reward ratio for cheating on taxes is favorable. They won't pay and funding for the government will dry up. It requires a huge, powerful, and well-armed police state agency, feared and loathed by the populace, equipped to use force, to collect the vast amount of revenue necessary to support the megastate.

But that's only one side of the equation. More than two-thirds of the U.S. budget is spent redistributing wealth. Wealth redistribution includes not just programs for the poor. It also includes social security, Medicare, and every other program that hands out money to large portions of the general population and to select groups. Beneficiaries of this redistribution include a variety of businesses, farmers, nonprofit organizations, contractors, banks, and Wall Street brokerage firms, anyone with the political clout to persuade powerful politicians to give them money. The welfare state also includes the costs of administering the huge agencies needed to accomplish the task, and the hundreds of billions of dollars inevitably lost to fraud, inefficiency, and waste.

Granting politicians the authority to decide from whom to take money, and to whom to give it, gives those politicians dominion over an unbounded field of power. The government hands out $3.8 trillion a year. Is it any surprise that Washington attracts special interests and lobbyists, looking for handouts, like sugar attracts ants? Vast armies of powerful men with money descend on Washington, the source of all power and money, in pursuit of the brass ring, hustling to get their share. In the last 15 years Washington became the wealthiest metropolitan area in the country, even as the rest of the nation descended into the great recession. People across the ideological spectrum believe that our political system is rotten to the core. They are right.

What those who worship at the altar of equality have to ask themselves is this: "Is it worth it?" When government power grows, the ambit of individual liberty correspondingly shrinks. How much liberty are you willing to surrender in the elusive quest for equality? When you hear politicians speak of compassion or social justice, hide your wallet.

Chapter 26

The Promised Land

"It's not that I'm afraid of dying. I just don't want to be there when it happens."
—**Woody Allen**

"Money can't buy friends, but you can get a better class of enemy."
—**Spike Milligan**

The good news for Samson and his crew was that they could see land in the distance. The bad news was that the engine was dead and the boat was taking on water. Fortunately they had life jackets, which they put on, took off their shoes, and jumped in the water. As the boat sank behind them, they swam for shore. It was a long, hard slog, but one by one, Delilah, Buddha, Pete, Isaac, and Samson swam ashore, pulled themselves out of the water, pulled off their life jackets, and collapsed exhausted on the Nassau beach. They paid no attention to the tourists who eyed them with suspicious curiosity.

They rested for a while, and when they had recuperated sufficiently, they walked into town, tired, hungry, wet, and disheveled. They found what they were looking for, a large bank building with a sign that read "International Bank of the Bahamas."

Pete and Isaac went to get something to eat while Samson, Delilah, and Buddha, still bedraggled, damp, and barefoot, entered the bank. They insisted on meeting with the bank president. Lower level officers, put off by their ragged appearance, said he was busy and would be unable to meet with them. "Tell him Sam Samson is here," Samson said. "And tell him I'm in a hurry."

The bank president, a Bahamian native with white hair and impeccably dressed in a white suit, came out to meet them, and apologized if there was any misunderstanding. They went into a conference room, and when they were seated around the table, the president asked, "You had a pleasant trip?"

"Actually, it was a little hectic," Samson answered, "you know—traveling."

"Yes, I was expecting you yesterday, actually."

"Well, our plane had some minor mechanical problems," Delilah explained. "And then we took a boat from Florida, and there were a couple of glitches with that too."

"Well, anyway," the president said. "I'm glad you made it. Welcome to the Bahamas."

"Did the bank wire arrive okay?" Samson asked, trying to sound casual.

"Yes, and was deposited in your secret account, as you instructed, Mr. Samson."

Samson, Delilah, and Buddha laughed with relief.

"And what was the exact amount of the deposit?" Samson asked.

The bank president looked at a stack of papers in front of him. "Seventeen point eight billion dollars, less a twenty-two dollar wire transfer fee."

"Seventeen point eight," Samson said.

"Correct."

"Million."

The bank president shook his head no, and looked down at the documents again. "That's *billion!*"

"Excuse me?" Samson asked.

"Billion," the president repeated. "Seventeen point eight billion."

"Dollars," Samson said.

Samson looked at Buddha with a "what the hell" look.

"Correct, seventeen point-eight billion dollars. Is something wrong, Mr. Samson?"

"No, that's what I was expecting," Samson said, clearing his throat. "I frequently deposit seventeen point eight billion."

"Yes," Delilah added. "I've seen him deposit seventeen point eight billion many times."

She moved closer to Samson, put her hand on his knee under the table and squeezed it in excitement.

"I'd say that makes you the twenty-seventh richest man in the world, Mr. Samson" the president said.

"Do you think you could waive that twenty-two dollar wire transfer fee?" Samson asked.

"No problem."

"Could you excuse us for a moment please?" Samson said. He stood up and put his hand on Buddha's shoulder, signaling that he needed to speak to him. Buddha stood up. Samson put his arm around Buddha's shoulder and walked him into a small adjoining room. Samson spoke in a semi-whisper. "Jesus, Buddha! You took seventeen point eight billion dollars? What the hell's wrong with you? Why so much?"

"Because it was there."

"Are you outta your mind? They'll be after us forever!"

"Yeah, but at least we'll have something to fight back with."

"All right, look," Samson said, "you're really the one who did this. Why don't you take half of it?"

"No thanks. I don't want them after *my* butt."

"Oh good."

"When the smoke clears, you can give me a cut."

"Yeah, sure, Buddha, when the smoke clears. But by then I may not feel so generous."

Samson and Buddha rejoined the others. "What do you recommend doing with the money?" Samson asked the president.

The president shuffled through the papers again. "As soon as the U.S. government releases its lien against the funds, you're free to use them," he said.

"Lien against the funds?"

"Yes, didn't you know?"

"Could I speak to you in private?" Samson asked. He and the president left the room and went into the president's office for a brief discussion.

When they came back into the conference room they were each carrying a stack of papers, and both were in high spirits as they shook hands. "Well, Mr. Samson, would you like me to work up an investment portfolio?" the president asked.

"You got the money released already, Sam?" Delilah asked.

Samson shrugged his shoulders and said, "Sure, why not."

Delilah closed her eyes and began undulating, going into an orgasmic spiritual reverie. She whispered something in Samson's ear.

"Is she okay?" the president asked. "She looks like she's having a religious experience."

"Yeah, she's very religious," Samson said.

The bank president took Samson by the arm and took him aside. He spoke in a hushed voice. "Mr. Samson, I must warn you. We've had unusual inquiries about these funds. You could be in grave danger. I can't talk about it."

"Don't talk about it."

Samson, Buddha, and Delilah emerged from the entrance of the bank into the street. The sun was setting, and the street was alive with tourists, merchants, and Caribbean music.

"How'd you get him to release the funds, Sam?" Buddha asked.

"I bought the bank."

Delilah leaned affectionately on Samson's arm. "Sam, have you ever thought about marriage?" she asked.

"Yeah. That's why I'm single."

"You took that line from Buster Keaton," Buddha said.

Chapter 27
Free At Last

"Never pick a fight with anyone who buys ink by the barrel."
—John F. Kennedy

*"Where there's smoke, there's someone with
a smoke making machine."*
—James Carville

Their troubles ostensibly behind them, and cash in their pockets, Samson and his crew did what anyone would have done under these circumstances. They checked into the biggest, gaudiest, glitziest five-star hotel in the Bahamas and reserved the most expensive suites in the place. They were exhausted, so the first night they all went to sleep early. But they'd been through a lot, so the next day they celebrated their escape, their triumph, and their new-found wealth. Pete, Isaac, and Buddha, attired in snazzy new suits they'd purchased that morning, met some good-looking women in the hotel bar, who were happy to join them in their suite for a lavish meal and party. After dinner, Samson and Delilah were out on the balcony enjoying the view.

Isaac came out hollering. "Sam, come take a look at this, quick!"

Samson and Delilah hurried back inside. A cable TV news broadcast from the United States was in progress. "We've had some delays in getting complete information," the newscaster said, "but our sources tell us that the entire IRS computer system has been wiped clean. The taxing agency has lost all programming, and all taxpayer records. A senior IRS spokesman said it could be years before the agency recovers from the cyber-attack, and in the meantime it will be impossible to collect taxes for an indeterminate period. IRS officials accuse escaped tax-evader Sam Samson of responsibility for the sabotage, which they are treating as a terrorist attack. They also accuse Samson of threatening to bomb dozens of federal office buildings, and stealing billions of dollars from the federal treasury and diverting it to his personal offshore bank account.

"In related news, millions of Americans have spontaneously taken to the streets in front of federal buildings in cities across the country, celebrating what some are calling 'tax freedom day.' But House Minority Leader Nancy Pelosi issued a press release saying that these demonstrations are not grass roots and spontaneous, but are what she calls 'astro turf,' artificially created by the Tea Party, with money provided by the Koch brothers, conservative billionaires who support anti-government activists. The public employee unions have issued press releases condemning the computer attack, and saying that their members will not work without pay, threatening a shutdown of the federal government."

On the TV, crowds of people jammed the streets, waved flags, set off fireworks, and cheered because they no longer had to pay taxes. Samson, Pete, and Isaac hooted and hollered, and gave each other "high fives."

But Delilah had a more subdued reaction. "Sam," she said, "you know this could turn ugly."

"What?"

"Think about what we just saw on TV. I mean, it's unbelievable that you escaped, got the money, and shut them down like that. It's amazing. And I don't wanna rain on the party. But you don't think this is over, do you?"

"No, I know. I've actually been thinking the same thing."

"Look at the way the press covered it: 'escaped tax evader, sabotage, terrorist attack, threatening to bomb federal buildings, stealing billions of dollars, offshore bank account.' Where do you think they're getting all this?"

"The government, I guess," Samson said.

"Exactly. They're making you look bad, Sam. You're gonna get the worst press since Osama Bin Laden, so when they kill you everyone'll be happy."

"I agree," Buddha chimed in. "Fortunately, however, there's something we can do about it."

"Well, we better do something," Delilah said, "cause I know how the agency works. They'll dig up dirt on you, and make you look like the biggest scumbag since Bernie Madoff. No, worse than Madoff. When the government PR machine puts out the word, the hacks in the media will turn against you in a heartbeat. By the time they're done, the public will think you're a no good, low down, crooked, tax-cheating, drug-dealing, mother-raping son of a bitch, and a traitor, to boot. You've got to get public opinion on your side, Sam, or you're going to get fried."

"Where we're going," Samson replied, "there is no public opinion."

"Sam, come on, get real. Do you think those people are gonna let this drop? They'll hunt you down wherever you are,"

Delilah said. "The good news is that you've got money; that gives you clout. You need to use it, and fight back. You need to win this battle in the United States or you're dead."

"Okay, you're right," Samson agreed. "What do you have in mind?"

• • •

Unbeknownst to Samson, Buddha had been secretly videotaping significant events, starting with Samson's closing argument and the disgraceful incident at the trial when juror # 1 was afraid to report jury tampering and pretended he had to go to the bathroom. With good editing, Buddha said, he could show the public how crooked IRS agents and a crooked judge had fixed the trial. He had the judge on tape, saying in front of the jury that Samson was "obviously guilty as hell," and other improprieties. He'd also recorded the shooting down of the plane, and the sinking of the boat, which would be portrayed as attempted murder by government thugs.

"Okay, Sam, here's the deal," Buddha continued. "You're the twenty-seventh wealthiest man in the world. You can operate on a level with the big boys, y'know, George Soros, the Koch Brothers, Warren Buffett, and the likes. Plus you've got me. I can launch an Internet campaign to get the truth out, social media, our own website, Facebook, YouTube, blogs, etcetera. I can even hack into government websites. From the Internet we can get it onto cable news, radio networks, magazines and newspapers. If *Time* magazine still exists we'll get you on the cover."

"He's right," Delilah said. "We can hire a big PR firm with the right media contacts, and lobbyists in Washington. We'll make you the most famous outlaw since Al Capone, and the most popular since Robin Hood."

"I don't care about being famous," Samson said.

"Look," Delilah answered. "If you get the American public on your side, politicians will follow public opinion and you'll be home free. The government won't be able to do anything to you. You're also going to need money to buy key members of Congress, and maybe even a few journalists. I worked in Washington for years. That's how it works. You'll be able to form alliances with politicians who will protect you. If you're not at the table, you're on the menu. The IRS is in disarray now. This is the time to strike."

"Okay," Samson said. "Very smart. So what do you need to make it happen, Buddha?"

"A budget," Buddha said.

"Okay, a budget" Samson said. "Submit a budget. You got it."

With Delilah's help, Buddha went to work, and within days, the media campaign was in full swing. They hired the top PR firms in Washington and New York, who made Sam Samson a household name, and lobbying firms with high-level congressional contacts. They spread money around. Controversy swirled around him, but this was made into an asset because it only generated more publicity. Samson made the cover of Time magazine, with a picture of him just before he boarded the plane the day he escaped. The title was "Tax Cheater Sam Samson: Hero or Villain?" There were powerful interests who hated Sam Samson, but to millions of Americans he became an anti-establishment folk hero in the tradition of Billy the Kid.

Chapter 28
The Grand Inquisitor

*"The Party seeks power entirely for its own sake.
We are not interested in the good of others;
we are interested solely in power, pure power."*
—George Orwell 1984

*"They've overturned the order of the soul,
give me absolute control, over every living soul,
I've seen the future, brother, it is murder."*
—Leonard Cohen

Samson's cyber-attack on the IRS, stealing of IRS money, and subsequent escape, was a national news story that had catapulted Samson's case from the obscurity of a routine "Plan for Universal Compliance" tax persecution into a major problem for the IRS. Elliott Mess was in hot water for bungling the case. The case evaluation report gave him high marks for the early stages of the case. He received grades of A+ in the following categories:

- Identification and surveillance of the target
- Gathering of evidence
- Seizure of all the target's assets to wipe him out financially (so he had no means of defending himself)

- Arrest and prosecution
- Outcome based intervention in the trial to assure conviction

However, fairly or unfairly, Mess received failing grades as a result of the following screw ups, although some of them, arguably, were not his fault:

- The target's success in acquiring cash, without detection by the IRS, cash that was used in his escape
- The target's escape from the courthouse with the assistance of ersatz guards in a stolen federal transport van
- The target's success at hacking into the IRS computer and theft of funds from the Treasury
- The target's theft of an IRS plane with the assistance of a co-opted undercover agent
- Mess's inability to capture or kill the target in the in-air and open sea confrontations
- The target's superior performance over the IRS in his post-incident online and media public relations blitz

Mess was called on the carpet by no less than the IRS commissioner himself. Elliot Mess stood in the commissioner's huge office in front of the commissioner's huge desk. The commissioner sat on the other side of that desk, reading the Case Evaluation Report in silence, as Mess stood there, holding his hat, waiting to find out his fate.

When he was done reading, the commissioner looked up at Mess, evaluating him visually, but said nothing, increasing

Mess's discomfort. Then he began tapping his pen impatiently on his desk, a clear indication of his dissatisfaction. Finally, he began to speak, choosing his words carefully. "Special Agent Mess, I don't need to state the obvious. I'm certain you understand that as the agent in charge of this case, you are accountable for every aspect of this disaster."

"Yes, sir," said Mess, who found himself overwhelmed by the commissioner's charismatic presence, and especially the extraordinary depth and resonance of his voice.

"Unfortunately," continued the commissioner, "you are also the person most familiar with the case and the most highly motivated to rectify it. How do you plan to do that?"

"Sir, I would like to draw one aspect of this matter to your attention. I don't want to make excuses, but we have a glitch in the enforcement system. Only *you* have the power to correct it. We were able to locate the target's escape boat with drone aircraft, controlled by the Department of Homeland Security. But DHS officials were uncooperative. They refused to use the drone to take out the target and his boat. This enabled him to escape and consummate his criminal assault on our computer network."

"Special Agent Mess," the commissioner responded, "that doesn't hold water. At the time of the boat incident you're referring to, the attack on our computer network had already been completed. You caught up with the target's small unarmed, motor boat on a fully armed coast guard ship, but were unable to apprehend or eliminate him. So I don't think the refusal to use the drone's smart bombs is an excuse for your failure. And if you don't get this guy and get this problem fixed, you're going to be demoted down to the Mattress Label Division, you got that?"

"The what?"

"The Mattress Label Division. Do you know what that is?"

"No sir."

"The Mattress Label Division, or MLD, is the federal bureau in charge of investigating alleged incidents of customers removing from mattresses labels which say 'it's a violation of federal law to remove this label.'"

"Yes, sir, I'll get him, sir."

"Having said that, I'm aware of the problem with the drones," the commissioner intoned. "And it will be corrected in Phase II, when control of the Department of Homeland Security, including the domestic drone program, will be centralized under our command. In fact, all the drones, domestic satellite spy and gps systems, video surveillance cameras, and face recognition programs in the country will be linked together, automated, coordinated, and centralized under our command. We'll know where everyone is at all times. This will enable us to keep track of all manner of anti-social misfits, malcontents, misanthropes, misogynists, dissenters, deviants, disbelievers, subversives, iconoclasts, anarchists, infidels, sodomites, traitors, terrorists, deadbeats, and n'er-do-wells throughout the country. If a transsexual goes into the wrong gender public bathroom, we'll know it."

"Excuse me, sir," Mess interrupted, "but which gender bathroom are transsexuals supposed to use?"

"We have a committee studying that very question as we speak. Keep in mind that there are many aspects to the Plan for Universal Compliance, and we're only in phase I. Actually, your target, Sam Samson, wreaked havoc on the Plan, throwing a monkey wrench into implementation. The entire Plan has been derailed for the time being. In fact, at present we're in retreat and survival mode, entirely as a result of *your* mishaps!" The commissioner pointed his index finger accusingly at Mess as he said these words, then repeatedly pounded his desk with the same finger, as if to drive home the point.

"Yes, commissioner, I understand the situation," Mess dared to interject, "but at this point, you've only disclosed phase I of the PUC. It would be helpful to me in completing my task if you could give me a brief overview now. I think you know how committed I am to the success of the Plan."

Mess was right; the commissioner did know how committed he was. He was generally circumspect and disclosed information about the Plan only on a "need to know" basis. But he had been aware of Elliott Mess's work at the agency for years, and despite his recent foul-ups, considered Mess to be one of his most loyal and effective agents. He would need key people under his command who understood the big picture, so he decided to take Mess into his confidence.

Although the commissioner would never have used such language to describe it, the Plan for Universal Compliance with the Code, was nothing less than a coup d'état, aimed at establishing a beneficent totalitarian regime in the United States, and ultimately, throughout the world, based on egalitarian principles. When the public thinks of a coup, they think of a swift power grab by the military in a dysfunctional banana republic. But such a simple coup would not be possible in a vast, democratic, cosmopolitan nation like the United States. There were complexities and moving parts in the American political economic system and the Plan would have to be implemented in phases, progressively taking control of one aspect of the system after another.

The media, of course, was oblivious. In every news story, there's always a huge gap between what is really going on and the superficial, simplistic media coverage. When it came to the Plan for Universal Compliance, the media didn't have a clue. As a result, the public was oblivious to the radical changes that were taking place beneath the surface of the American polity.

The architects of the Plan recognized the enormity of their task. Earlier totalitarians didn't seize power in one fell swoop either. Stalin, Hitler, Saddam Hussein, the Mullahs in Iran, had to build and consolidate their power in stages. It would be easy to dismiss the IRS commissioner as a delusional kook, obsessed with the insane belief that he was going to take over the United States, and then go on to, dare I say it, rule the world. Although it may have been true that the commissioner was a fruitcake, that didn't mean he wouldn't succeed. In point of fact, the most successful totalitarian dictators have all been megalomaniacal lunatics with delusions of grandeur; the commissioner fit the profile perfectly.

And the commissioner had three other things working in his favor. For one thing, the United States had been moving further and further in the direction of a nonconstitutional centralized government bureaucracy for decades. Make a few modest changes, such as centralizing control of information, elections, and the money supply, and you're most of the way there. Second, the commissioner had a network of powerful allies at the levers of power in Congress, throughout the executive branch bureaucracy; at the Federal Reserve; at the highest level of foreign countries, including Russia, China, Germany, and France; and at international institutions including The World Bank and International Monetary Fund. Third, he had a strong intuitive understanding of American politics and a brilliant plan. He may have been crazy, but he wasn't stupid.

"All right, Special Agent Mess," the commissioner began, "would you like to be part of a force greater than yourself? And will you pledge your personal loyalty to me and your life to support this cause?"

Mess nodded.

"Although we've suffered a temporary setback due to the sabotage of your Mr. Samson," the commissioner continued, "the big picture is that we are on the brink of an historic transformation, not only of the United States, but of the entire world's political economic system. This can best be understood in the context of economic history. Capitalism is a flawed system because it creates vast inequalities in wealth, and offends universal sensibilities about social justice. However, as an economic system, capitalism is indispensable. Only capitalism can transform a primitive traditional society into an advanced modern economy. In the early stages of societal transformation, capitalist incentives produce the technologies that create wealth, and power is widely disbursed. Entrepreneurs are predominant, and government maintains a low profile. But when the level of wealth created by capitalism reaches critical mass, government begins to seize that wealth, and use it for its own purposes. However, government appropriation of wealth is a risky business. If the government over-reaches it can kill the goose that laid the golden egg. Communism failed because it destroyed capitalism. Without market capitalism, the communist system was unable to perform the basic functions of a modern economy.

"We won't make that mistake. We will keep capitalism alive, but subordinate it to our purposes. The masses will support our policy, recognizing that the purpose of capitalism isn't to make individuals rich, but to serve the state, the state which collectively embodies the will of the people. The state in turn will take care of the needs of the people. And this is the ultimate fulfillment of democracy. This is how equality becomes a reality. The masses will support us because they despise inequality, which elevates a select few to the level of demigods, while the masses are left at the bottom, wallowing in feelings of inferiority and resentment.

"Equality can only be achieved through the government's exercise of its power to take wealth from those who would prefer to keep it. Even more daunting is the other side of the equation, deciding who gets the money. This vast exercise of power must be executed by those who won't be corrupted by the power. To achieve peace and equality, the masses must understand that the power at our command is being used for their benefit. If we give them material security, they will willingly surrender their freedom."

"Sir," Elliott Mess interjected, "I've been waiting my entire life for a leader to say what you've just said. It reflects everything I've always believed, and I want to affirm that I'm with you all the way."

"Okay, now getting to the nuts and bolts," the commissioner resumed. "There are three phases of the Plan. In phase one, we consolidate control of government revenue. We project that our plan will increase tax collections by twenty-five percent in the first year. In the second part of phase one, cash will cease to be recognized as currency in the United States. Going to a cashless financial system will be presented as a way to stop drug dealer and terrorist money laundering, and shut down organized crime. In the future, all financial transactions will be conducted digitally, and cleared through a central federal agency, which we will control. This information will be included in the data stored at our new million-square foot, data-mining hard drive center in Utah, where, even as we speak, our computer hard drives are collecting complete data on every man, woman, and child in America. We will know every nickel spent or received by every person or business entity in the United States. Tax evasion and other types of for-profit criminal activity will become impossible. Individuals like Sam Samson, operating anonymously in the shadows of society, will be a thing of the past.

"The additional funds collected, nearly a trillion dollars annually, will be funneled into a special fund for implementation of the Plan, and creation of a new nonvisible layer of government. The invisible government will include a secret domestic police force, in effect, a private army, and will establish our control of the command centers of key federal institutions.

"In phase two, in the name of curbing political corruption, all special interest and private funding of political campaigns will be prohibited. All campaign funding will be provided by us. We will thus gain control of both major political parties. The public will be told by the media that we have entered a new era of social harmony in which political dissension has been replaced by bipartisan harmony. Both parties will finally come to work together for the common good. The masses will think this is wonderful.

"Phase two will also include a new media regulatory commission. All news and commentary will be prescreened. Only information that the commission determines to be fair and objective will be reported. The Internet will also be brought under regulation. This regulation will be sold to the public as necessary to prevent false information from being spread by America's enemies, and to stop hacking, and cyber-attacks that threaten national security. The residual print media is anachronistic and will be phased out. Regulation of the media will give us monopolistic dissemination of information, and will suppress subversion and dissent.

"In phase three, we will assume digital control of all elections and ballot counting, thereby consolidating control of the political system. This will eliminate the negative campaigning and conflicts that have offended voters and corrupted the political process in the past. We will work with our allies at the Federal Reserve to nationalize all banks. This will give us total control of the money supply and centralized dominion over the social order."

"How will we deal with groups who oppose us, sir?" Mess interjected. "Y'know, like those so called 'limited government' or 'anti-tax' or 'constitutionalist' groups?"

"Those people are anachronisms, and the public will be turned against them. They'll have no media to promulgate their out-of date-ideology. Any hold-outs who refuse to renounce those ideas will be put in 're-education camps.' Such notions will be wiped out like small pox.

"Now, understand, Special Agent Mess," the commissioner continued. "The information I've given you is to be kept confidential. If you breathe a word to anyone, I will have you terminated."

"Terminated in the sense of laid off?" Mess asked.

"No, terminated in the sense of terminated, as in the Schwarzenegger sense of no longer existing. Now getting back to our immediate problem, what to do with Mr. Sam Samson."

"Why don't we just kill him, sir?"

"No, it's too late for that, not after this public relations nightmare. We don't want to make a martyr out of him. Keep his body alive. But bring him to me. We'll make an example of him. We'll crush his spirit, and force him to publicly recant. He'll just *wish* he was dead." As the commissioner spoke, his words were interspersed with the sound of air passing through a tube.

Elliott Mess was a stoic, a master at subduing and concealing his emotions. But the Plan embodied everything he believed in and held sacred. He was inspired by the commissioner's vision of a world where people who understood power, and knew how to use it, people like – him – would finally be in charge. He was excited by the opportunity to play an important role in fundamentally transforming America. He was so inspired that he no longer felt troubled by the commissioner's peculiar attire. Mess now understood why the commissioner wore a cape and a helmet covering his face. As the commissioner uttered the words "crush his spirit," Mess felt a thrill down his leg as he realized that the commissioner didn't just *dress* like Darth Vader; for all intents and purposes he *was* Darth Vader, the only distinction being that his cape was purple.

"Lord Vader—" Mess found himself saying.

"No, not Vader," the commissioner interrupted. "Nader. Darth Nader."

"Sorry, Lord...Nader, what does the president think?"

"Whatever I tell him to think," the commissioner said. This was a slight exaggeration.

Dubious Philosophical Musings

Part VIII

Greed Is Good

"A major source of objection to a free economy is precisely that it ... gives people what they want instead of what a particular group thinks they ought to want. Underlying most arguments against the free market is a lack of belief in freedom itself."
—Milton Friedman

"World War II was the last government program that really worked."
—George Will

Human beings like to acquire stuff. We like to go to market places, stores, swap meets, auctions, and garage sales. We like to make money. Money is a store of value that enables us to acquire more stuff. Why are we like this? It's evolution. Cavemen were hunters and gatherers. They acquired food and saved it for the winter. The cavemen who weren't into acquiring and saving stuff died and didn't reproduce. Cave *women* had no interest in cave *men* who weren't into hunting and acquiring and didn't want to mate with such men. Cavemen who weren't acquisitive not only had difficulty finding a mate, but if they did find one, they didn't do a good job of providing for their offspring. So their offspring died, and those nonacquisitive genes weren't passed on. Those who were acquisitive by nature flourished, got the girl, reproduced, supported their offspring, and passed those acquisitive genes onto their descendants—i.e us. That's why we like to acquire money. We inherited the acquisitive gene from our acquisitive reproductively successful cavemen ancestors.

Free market capitalism recognizes and exploits this acquisitive aspect of human nature (which some people denigrate with the pejorative term "greed") to create the incentive system which built the technology on which modern civilization is based. Gordon Gekko (the Michael Douglas character in the movie *Wall Street*) was right: "Greed is good." Greed discovered fire. Greed invented the wheel and the microchip. Greed took us to the moon; it will take us to the stars.

Unlike capitalism, socialism tries to suppress human acquisitiveness and the pursuit of self-interest, a futile quest. Socialism is oppression because it is incompatible with human nature. In the long term all socialist systems decay from the ongoing strain of trying to control natural human behavior, and ultimately collapse.

Chapter 29

As Good As It Gets

"One should forgive one's enemies, but not before they are hanged."
—**Heinrich Heine**

"I just sit here so patiently waiting to find out what price, you have to pay to keep from going through all of these things twice."
—**Bob Dylan**

On a Caribbean island, a private paradise with white sands and palm trees, Samson and his crew were on the beach, in bathing suits, enjoying the sunshine and turquoise waters. Samson sat in a lounge chair with a cigar in one hand and a drink in the other, Delilah at his side. The other guys were laughing with some beautiful Caribbean women. A live Reggae band played in the background.

"We did it, Sam," Delilah said. "It doesn't get any better than this, does it?"

"I'm so tired of fighting," Samson said. "Thank God, we can finally get some peace and quiet."

As he said these words, the music and laughing suddenly stopped. Everyone fell silent as a military ship, as if out of nowhere, came into the dock. Elliott Mess and seven other armed agents emerged from the ship, put on their sunglasses, and came up on the beach. Everyone froze in place. Seeing Mess, Samson looked at his cigar and hurriedly put it out in the sand.

"That asshole's like 'the Terminator,'" Isaac said. "He keeps coming back."

The agents surrounded Samson, but he calmly remained seated, with his hand prominently on Delilah's thigh just to irritate Mess. Mess stood over Samson, blocking the sunlight and casting a shadow over him. "Stand up, Samson," Mess said. "We're taking you back to prison in the United States."

"No you're not," Samson said, not moving.

Two other agents moved toward Samson, as did Mess, and were about to forcibly lift him out of the lounge chair.

"You can't do that, Agent Mess," Samson said. "We don't have an extradition treaty with the United States."

"Nonsense," Mess retorted. "The United States and the Bahamas have had an extradition treaty for fifty years."

"This isn't the Bahamas."

"Nice try, Samson, but I know this island belongs to the Bahamas." He grabbed Samson by the shoulder and elbow, as the other two agents grabbed his other arm.

"It *did* belong to the Bahamas," Samson said, swinging his arms free of the agents' grasp. "I bought it last week. Our secretary of state here has the proof."

Isaac stepped up with a file containing some official-looking documents. The startled agents let go their grasp of Samson as Isaac showed the documents to Mess. "That's right, Agent Mess," said Isaac. "Here's the deed of title. Here's our constitution. You are standing in the free and independent nation of Samsonia. Sam Samson is our duly-elected president. So please get your ass outta here."

Mess grabbed the documents out of Isaac's grasp, tore them up, and threw them on the ground. "It doesn't work, Samson," Mess said. He took off his sunglasses, folded them, and put them in his inside jacket pocket. "You think you can buy land with money you stole from the United States and start your own country?"

"Yeah," said Samson.

"Hey," Isaac objected. "Desecrating our founding documents is a crime here in Samsonia. You're in big trouble, pal."

Mess ignored him. "No, Samson. You have to give the money back."

"I don't give money back," Samson said.

"Well you can tell that to the judge." Mess brandished his gun as his men grabbed Samson and lifted him roughly out of the chair. Mess put his gun to Samson's head.

"Hey Mess," Samson said. "How come you always wear that stupid 1930s hat and overcoat, even in the tropics?"

"You're under arrest, wise-aleck," Mess said.

"No, Agent Mess," Samson answered. "*You're* under arrest!" Twenty-five Caribbean uniformed men, Samsonia guards, armed with automatic weapons, suddenly moved in behind Mess and his men, seemingly from out of nowhere, and surrounded the IRS agents.

Pete stepped forward. "Drop your weapons," he said to the IRS agents. The Samsonia guards relieved Mess's men of their weapons. Samson sat down again in his lounge chair, re-lit his cigar, and put his hand back on Delilah's thigh. Pete stood in front of Mess, face to face, as the Samsonia guards handcuffed Mess and his men.

"Agent Mess," Pete continued. "I am chief of national security for the nation of Samsonia. You and your men are under arrest for launching an armed assault on our peace-loving nation, for desecrating our founding documents, and for the attempted abduction of our president. You do not have a right to an attorney. We have no attorneys in Samsonia, and we don't intend to allow any in. You do have a right to remain silent. I hope you *will* remain silent; I'm tired of hearing you speak. You will be granted a fair and impartial trial. And when your trial is over, I'm gonna hang you."

"You took that line from Marlon Brando," Isaac said.

"No, Karl Malden," Pete answered.

"Marlon Brando. In 'One Eyed Jacks,'" Isaac insisted.

"No, Karl Malden said it *to* Marlon Brando."

Pete and Isaac continued this argument as they, along with Samson, accompanied the Samsonia guards, marching Mess and his men across the beach, off to the guardhouse.

Realizing that the argument about who the line came from wasn't going well, Isaac changed the subject. "Are you really Jewish, Pete?" he asked. Pete nodded. "Funny, you don't look Jewish. You look like an Indian."

"I was born into the Sioux Nation," Pete said.

They reached the guardhouse, and the guards put Mess's men in one unit, and Mess himself in a separate unit.

"How'd you wind up being Jewish?" Isaac asked.

"My father sent me to a Jewish summer camp in Maine—Camp Takaho. He thought it was for Indians."

"He should have sent you to Camp Goldberg," Samson inserted. "That's where the Indian kids went."

Chapter 30
Reversal of Fortune

"Hell hath no fury like a bureaucrat scorned."
—**Milton Friedman**

*"It went on yesterday, and it's going on tonight.
Somewhere there's somebody
ain't treating somebody right."*
—**Bob Seger**

The next morning, Samson had workmen begin building a hanging gallows, visible to Mess and his men through the barred windows of the guard house. An armed Samsonia guard sentry stood guard outside the door. As the work was nearing completion, Samson went to see Mess in the guard house. The guard unlocked the cell and let him in. Pete and the guard waited outside. Samson stood looking down at Mess, who was sitting on a bench, but didn't say anything.

Mess broke the silence. "You've won this battle, Samson," he said, "but you know you can't win the war. If you'd just escaped, you might have gotten away. But you had to be a wise-ass, and wipe out our computers."

"You're just jealous 'cause Delilah likes me better."

Mess stood up. "That gold-digging slut means nothing to me. And how long do you think she'll stick around after the money's gone, which could be any day now? And as for you, you may be a hero today, but the masses have a short memory. But the government doesn't. How do you think your 'Samsonia' guards'll stack up against a Marine division? You think you're gonna hang a treasury officer and then just go on with your life?"

"I'm not gonna hang you, Mess."

"No?"

"No. I don't hang people."

"So what's that for?" Mess asked, pointing out the window.

"In case I change my mind." Samson turned his back on Mess and looked out the window at the gallows. The work was finished and a workman was testing it. He hung a sack of concrete from the rope and opened the trap door. The rope fell down, the sack of concrete broke open, and the contents spilled out. Mess turned away, but Samson kept looking out the window. "I'll find some other way to settle the score."

"Settle the score for what?"

Samson spun around and faced Mess. "For what? You steal my money, punch me in the face, take my house, seize my business, arrest me, rig my trial, shoot down my plane…"

"That wasn't your plane," Mess objected.

"Let's not get bogged down in legal technicalities. I was in the plane; you shot it down. Then you sink my boat and come after me on my own island with guns. And call my girlfriend a gold-digging slut?"

"She *is* a gold-digging slut! I guess you don't mind sloppy seconds." Mess was not accustomed to being in a subservient position. And given his present circumstance, this wasn't a very diplomatic thing to say. Maybe it was Mess's crude comment, or maybe Samson was just looking for an excuse. He hauled off and punched Mess in the face, giving him a black eye and knocking him down. The tables were clearly turned, as Samson stood over Mess in a manner reminiscent of the way Mess had stood over him the first time they met.

"Well, now," Samson said, "looks like I've given *you* a receipt."

Mess, still lying on his back, suddenly kicked Samson in the groin. Samson bent over in pain. Mess jumped up, grabbed a plate left from his lunch, which was sitting on the bench, and hit Samson on the back of the head with it. Samson punched Mess in the stomach. As they fought, Pete and the guard rushed into the room. The guard was about to break it up and grab Mess, but Pete held him back. "Let them have it out," he said.

Mess and Samson continued this knock-down fight, with first one having the advantage, then the other. Finally, Samson was left standing, panting heavily. Mess, also panting heavily, had gotten the worst of it, as demonstrated by the fact that he was lying on the floor. Samson turned toward the door to leave, but Mess tripped him with his foot and Samson fell down. With his last ounce of strength Mess punched him one more time in the face, and Samson punched Mess one more time in the face. But both men were now too out of breath to continue the brawl. They lay flat on their backs next to each other, exhausted, panting, staring at the ceiling.

"Hey, Pete," Samson said, "next time I'm in a fight, feel free to jump in and help."

Pete stood, his legs shoulder width apart, looking over them, his hands folded in front of him. "That wouldn't be fair," he said.

"It's true it wouldn't be fair," Samson agreed, "but do it anyway."

Chapter 31
All the King's Men

"A moderate is someone who takes an opinion poll on the question 'Should cannibalism be legalized?' and checks 'no opinion/don't know.'"
—**Ann Coulter**

"Iff you want a friend in Washington, get a dog."
—**Harry Truman**

The president of the United States sat at his desk in the oval office, talking to his top political consultant/pollster, Karl Rogue, who sat across the desk from him.

"Mr. President," Rogue said, "your approval numbers are in the toilet. Unless we do something to turn it around, you're going to have your head handed to you in November."

"No shit, Karl," the president said. "So tell me something I *don't* know. Like, for example, how come if you're so smart, like the media says, you haven't figured out a way to make me popular yet?"

"Actually, I have, Mr. President. How about this? You know that guy who shut down the IRS?"

"Yeah, Sam Samson. Don't worry about him. We'll have him in custody in two days."

"That would be a big mistake."

"Mistake? Are you nuts? That sonofabitch practically destroyed the government!"

"Yeah, that may be, but unlike you, sir, he's extremely popular. We just got poll numbers showing seventy-six percent of voters are glad the IRS was shut down, including people who don't even pay taxes. Seventy-eight percent of voters have a positive view of Sam Samson, and sixty-eight percent say he's a national hero."

"Hmm. That sucks. Okay, okay. But if I don't arrest him, the IRS commissioner'll kill me."

"*Arrest* him? Are you listening to me? Look, you can destroy that meglomaniac psycho IRS Commissioner Darth Nader, or whatever the hell he calls himself, restore our republic, win a place in history, and win the election—all in one fell swoop."

"What the hell are you talking about, Karl? You remember what happened the last time I tried to cross Darth Nader? He threatened to release all that tax info about me and accuse me of cheating on taxes. It doesn't pay to go against that guy; he's got too much power."

"Look, Mr. President. Remember back in the old days when presidents used to be afraid of J. Edgar Hoover, the FBI director, for the same reason? He used to blackmail them. Then it turned out he liked wearing women's clothes. It's the same deal with Darth Nader. It's not just the purple cape. We've got videos the idiot sent to young interns showing himself parading around in pink panties."

"Man, how'd you get the videos?"

"How do you think? Just be glad I'm on your side. Anyway, now that Nader's computer system's been shut down, he doesn't have the info to blackmail you anymore. The guy's been declawed. This is the time to strike, while he's weak, and bring that stupid bastard down."

"Okay, okay, fine, so what's your plan? How we do all this, y'know, what you said, bring down Nader, win the election, my place in history, and all that?" the president asked.

"Instead of destroying Sam Samson, honor him as a national hero. Get him on our team, wrap yourself in his popularity, and show up Darth Nader as the whack job villain he is"

"Ya think?"

"Yeah, I think."

"Yeah, okay. Brilliant idea. Glad I thought of it."

The next day a helicopter flew over the island of Samsonia, and swooped down to land. By the time it hit the ground it was surrounded by several armed crack Samsonian guard troops. A well-groomed, trim, forty-something man in an expensive suit, carrying a brief case, stepped out, holding his hat so the wind from the helicopter wouldn't blow it off. The guards saw that other than the pilot, who remained on board, the man was the only one on the helicopter. They swarmed around him, patted him down and found he was unarmed, so they lowered their weapons. Samson heard the noise and came out of his exercise room, clad in a bathing suit and tennis shoes, pumped up from his work out, glistening with sweat, a towel around his neck. He watched the man from a distance, and signaled to the guards to let him through. The man strode up to Samson confidently. "Sam Samson?" he said. "My name is John Keister. I work for the president of the United States. Is there somewhere we can talk in private?"

"Step into my office," Samson said, and showed John Keister to the poolside patio behind his house. They sat down by a table in the shade of an umbrella, mounted on a pole that was stuck through a hole in the center of the table. A servant brought them cold beverages as they talked.

"Mr. Samson," John Keister began, "the president wants to help you."

"The president…"

"Yes."

"Of the United States."

"Yes."

"Wants to help me."

"Correct."

"Well why didn't he help me when those bastards were rigging my trial and shooting down my plane?"

"Well, to be honest…." John Keister said….

"I mean at that point, I could have used some help," Samson interrupted. "At this point, Mr., uh, sorry—what did you say your name was?"

"Keister. John Keister."

"Yeah, at this point, Mr. Keister, look around. Does it look like I need help?"

"Looks can be deceiving."

"Okay, I don't want to deal in riddles. Why don't you just tell me what you want?"

"It's not what I want. It's what the president wants."

"Okay, how about you tell me what the president wants."

"Okay, Mr. Samson. I do special jobs for the president. I meet with him in person; I don't go through an intermediary. You will not find my name or job title anywhere in government records. My salary is not included in the budget of any department. I handle discreet matters for the president behind the scenes."

"How do I know that you are who you say you are?"

"Here is my business card, Mr. Samson." He handed Samson a plain white card with nothing on it except the name "John Keister" and two phone numbers. "The first number is my private cell phone. The second number is the White House switchboard. If you call the White House switchboard and ask for me, they will not know who I am. However, if we come to terms today, I will provide you with a code and the name of a secretary who works in the White House who will be able to put you through to me. Then you'll know who I am."

"Okay, I'm listening."

"Okay, you may have begun to suspect as a result of, um, I know you've had some unfortunate experiences over the past several months, so you've probably sensed that something isn't quite, uh, normal, if you catch my drift. There are forces at work in the public sector, which are, so to speak, operating below the surface. I'll be quite frank with you. There has been a power struggle of titanic proportions going on in Washington that the public is unaware of. Although you probably didn't have an inkling what was going on, you stumbled into the middle of that struggle. Your little computer maneuver against the IRS altered the dynamics of that power conflict in a way that could change history."

"Well, that's a fascinating story, Mr. Keister, and it doesn't really surprise me because, to tell you the truth, I came across some weird shit that was going on. Having said that, however, why, at this point, should I give a damn what happens in the United States?"

"Well, that's understandable, but unfortunately, you may be willing to forget the United States, but the United States isn't willing to forget you. You put yourself in the middle of something big, and well, frankly, you've become a player."

"I don't wanna be a player."

"Well, what you want doesn't have a whole lot do with it. Why don't you let me explain the situation, and then you can decide what role you'd like to play? You know, your little cyber-attack on the IRS, combined with your clever PR campaign, made you quite popular in some circles. And frankly, it's impressive how quickly you figured out how to use money the way it's intended to be used."

"Yeah, that's right," Samson answered. "If I keep this up I might degenerate into one of those crony capitalist sons of bitches."

"Look, those crony capitalist sons of bitches pay my salary," Keister replied, "so I've got nothing bad to say about them. But in any case, the point is that you've done a great job with the media. But if you dig deeper into the polling, it's more nuanced. Taxpayers hate the IRS and they thought what you did was cool, but not everyone pays taxes. And among both groups, taxpayers and nontaxpayers, even among those who were glad you took out the IRS computer system, solid majorities condemned you for stealing taxpayer money."

"Look, I just took the money so I'd have the means to protect myself. I didn't start this war. The IRS started it. They stole *my* money. I stole *their* money. I'd say it's a wash."

"Oh, I agree with you, Mr. Samson. Morally and tactically, your actions were fully justified. But that's really beside the point."

"Okay, so what *is* the point?"

"The point is public perception. The public tends to look at these kinds of issues simplistically. And the perception is that on the one hand you're a great guy, with the balls to fight the IRS; but on the other hand you're a thief, who stole taxpayer money."

"Okay, so where are we going with all this?"

"The president wants to help you, but he needs something in return."

"He wants to help me what? And what makes you think I need help? Did you know I'm the twenty-seventh richest man in the world?"

"Actually you're now the twenty-sixth richest. Some Russian mogul had some currency speculation go against him last week."

"Whatever."

"Well, anyway, there's a fundamental problem that may or may not have occurred to you."

"Uh-huh."

"The U.S. government has a policy against allowing people to steal its money, y'know, unless authorized by Congress."

"Yeah, so?"

"So you can't keep the money."

"That's what you flew down here to tell me?"

"No, it's more complicated than that. The president wants you to be his friend."

"Why, is he lonely?"

"No, he has interns if he gets lonely. He wants to help you."

"Yeah, you already said that. Help me what?"

"Help you stay alive."

"Uh-huh."

"Help you stay out of prison."

"Uh-huh."

"Help you stay out of the hands of dangerous, vicious people, who will do you grave harm if they get a hold of you."

"Okay, you got my attention. And, forgive my cynicism, but could you please explain why the president of the United States wants to help me?"

"Mr. Samson, your destruction of the IRS computer system came at an auspicious time. You inadvertently prevented a coup d'état that came very close to toppling the government of the United States. And that struggle is still going on. I take it you don't trust the president, and maybe you don't have a high opinion of him, but let me tell you, he is on the right side of this struggle. And if he goes down, the forces of darkness will win, and the entire world will be at risk. Now you may not give a damn about your country anymore, and to be honest, I can't say as I blame you, but if you give a damn about yourself, you damn well better hope the good guys win."

"So what do you want?"

"If you agree to certain conditions, the president will pardon you of all crimes. You'll be free to return to the United States, if you choose. You'll be treated as a national hero, and certain other benefits will accrue to you. You will be a friend of the president, for your mutual benefit, and under his protection, which is the best chance you have of surviving. Your status as a hero will help the president achieve his political goals, including defeating the dark forces of totalitarianism he is fighting."

"Okay, I got the picture. I'll think it over and get back to you."

"One other thing. You must maintain confidence. You are not to discuss the contents of this conversation with anyone. That means *anyone*. Understood?"

"Understood."

Chapter 32
Independence Day

"My reading of history convinces me that most bad government results from too much government."
—**Thomas Jefferson**

*"Do not dress in those rags for me;
I know you are not poor.
And don't love me quite so fiercely
now when you know you are not sure.*
—**Leonard Cohen**

The president of the United States, two American flags behind him, one on either side, stood behind a lectern in the Capitol Building, before a specially called joint session of Congress, making a televised speech to the nation.

"My fellow Americans," he said. "For the first time since the Civil War, our nation is in the midst of a constitutional crisis. Until tonight, you have been kept in the dark, but it is time for the truth to be told. The leaders of the American Revolution believed that men are endowed by their Creator with certain unalienable rights. But a counterrevolution has inexorably expanded the power of the central government, overburdened our people with oppressive taxes, and usurped the liberty of our citizens. The forces of despotism are trying to take over America. But I give you my pledge tonight that I will not let this happen."

IRS Commissioner Darth Nader sat in the front row, surrounded by IRS agents, glowering at the president, unaware that the TV cameras were broadcasting his scowl to the nation.

"Our nation," the president continued, "has been sinking into an Orwellian police state with despotic central power. These whack jobs want to take over the whole world. And frankly, I'm getting sick of taking orders from some heavy breathing science fiction head case who thinks he's Darth Vader."

At these words, Darth Nader stridently stood up and stormed out, his purple cape flowing prominently behind him, followed by his entourage of IRS special agents in trench coats and black hats. Members of Congress and the press scurried to get out of his way as he tromped through. All of this was shown on TVs throughout the nation and the world. The president watched this move, shook his head yes, and gave a thumbs up.

"But there's one great patriot," the president went on, "chosen by God, who had the courage to stand up to these despots. Our nation owes a debt of gratitude and honor to Sam Samson. Time Magazine raised the question about this brave man, whether he was a hero or villain. Well, I'm here tonight to answer that question. Sam Samson is a hero."

Among the millions of people watching this historic speech on television were Samson and Delilah, lying in bed still on their Caribbean island, Samson in a bathrobe, Delilah in a negligee by his side.

"Sam, this is so exciting," she said. "You're a national hero." She snuggled up to him affectionately.

"Sam Samson risked his life to free his country," the president continued. "And let me clarify something that may have troubled some of you. There have been allegations from some quarters that Sam Samson appropriated money from the U.S. Treasury and used it for his own purposes. But the truth is that he only borrowed that money because rogue IRS agents rigged his trial. He only took as much as he needed to escape this injustice, and by mutual agreement, he will be returning to the U.S. Treasury the full amount that was taken."

"Did you hear that?" Delilah said to Samson, pulling away from him suddenly.

"What?" Samson replied.

"What he just said. That you're giving the money back. What's that about, Sam?" Her eyes flashed with fire.

"I don't know."

"Well is it true? Are you giving the money back? Why would he say that? "

"He's a politician. Politicians lie. I don't know." Delilah remained suspicious and stubbornly distant toward him for the rest of the night.

"I am hereby granting Sam Samson a full pardon," the president continued, "and ordering the FBI to investigate the IRS agents who have been harassing him. Pending the outcome of that investigation, I am demoting IRS Special Agent Elliott Mess to the Showerhead and Toilet Division of the Environmental Protection Agency. Elliot Mess's duties will be limited to investigating allegations that citizens have tampered with their showerheads to exceed federal environmental regulations that permit a maximum showerhead water flow of two point five gallons per minute. Special Agent Mess will also be assigned to investigate violations of the Energy Policy Act of nineteen ninety-two by suspects who are alleged to have toilets that use more than one point six gallons of water per flush. This is not to minimize the seriousness of these violations of federal law. But at least in his new assignment Special Agent Mess will not have the power to violate the rights of American taxpayers."

Elliott Mess, who still had a black eye, was sitting at home on his couch brushing his teeth, in his usual 1930's coat and hat, watching the speech. The doorbell rang. When he went to answer it, toothpaste dripping down his chin, he was confronted by two FBI agents. They came in and began questioning him. "Frankly, Special Agent Mess, we don't like having to do this. We think you got a raw deal. But you know the winds in Washington are shifting again. The good news is that we think we can keep you out of the penitentiary, and in fact, someone's pulled a few strings for you, which has enabled us to find you other federal employment."

"Doing what?" Mess asked.

"Well the best option might be one of the new openings in the Energy Department. The Department has a new Light Bulb Investigative Unit – very exciting work, from what I understand."

"The what?" Mess asked.

"Light Bulb Investigative Unit or LBIU. This is the latest thing in federal oversight. A lotta buzz about it."

"What do they do?"

"They're in charge of enforcement of 'The Energy Independence and Security Act of two thousand seven.' This is the unit that investigates allegations of suspects using outlawed incandescent light bulbs in their homes instead of federally mandated energy-saving compact fluorescents. Like I say, very exciting work. This is the way of the future, Special Agent Mess, not like that Mattress Label Unit, that you may have been considering. That one's a graveyard."

"Look, I think I'll just keep going after Sam Samson."

"You don't understand," said the FBI Agent.

"No, *you* don't understand!" said Mess, slamming his hand on the table.

"I'm trying to tell you, you can't work for the IRS anymore."

"Then it doesn't matter," said Mess. "Then I'll be around in the dark. I'll be everywhere —wherever you look…."

"You took that line from John Steinbeck," interrupted the Agent.

"Wherever Sam Samson removes a mattress label, I'll be there," Mess continued. "Wherever he goes through a red light, I'll be there. If he doesn't pay for his parking meter, or downloads a copyrighted video, I'll be there. Wherever he makes a large cash deposit or forgets to file a ten ninety-nine form, I'll be there. If he remodels his house without a permit, I'll be there. Whatever he does, I'll be watching. If he drives a car, I'll tax the street. If he tries to sit, I'll tax his seat. If he gets too cold, I'll tax the heat. If he takes a walk, I'll tax his feet. Don't ask me what I want it for, if you don't want to pay some more. Cause I'm the taxman. Yeah, I'm the taxman. And you're working for no one but me.'"

"Very impressive," said the FBI agent.

"Yeah, did you notice how seamlessly he went from Steinbeck to the Beatles?" said the other Agent. Both agents thought Mess had lost his mind.

Their conversation was slightly distracted by Mess's TV, on which the president continued his speech. "In the months since

Sam Samson effectively put the IRS out of business," the president was saying, "the American people and businesses have been freed from the burdens of the income tax. The result of this massive tax cut? Economic production and employment have soared, and our economy is now growing faster than it has for three generations. I therefore today introduced in Congress legislation to permanently abolish the Internal Revenue Service, repeal the income tax, and restore to the American people the freedom that is our birthright."

As the president completed these words, thanks to the work of Karl Rogue, a video was inserted into the president's presentation and seen on TVs throughout the world of what appeared to be a humongous spontaneous cheer in response to the president's message, coming from across America. Then American flags waving in the wind, footage of marines raising the flag at Iwo Jima, as "God Bless America" played. There were 4th of July fireworks, throngs of happy people celebrating, parades, waving flags, and cheering throughout the land. The famous footage of Saddam Hussein's statue being toppled, the Berlin wall coming down, culminating with footage of Martin Luther King's famous speech: "Free at last, free at last, thank God almighty, I'm free at last!"

The television networks had no idea how Rogue had pulled off inserting all this extraneous video footage into their broadcasts, but Buddha had had a hand in it, and even media pundits who hated Karl Rogue later conceded it was a major public relations coup.

Chapter 33
Gone With the Wind

"Politics is the art of looking for trouble, finding it everywhere, diagnosing it incorrectly, and applying the wrong remedies."
—**Groucho Marx**

*"Your eyes are soft with sorrow.
Hey, that's no way to say goodbye."*
—**Leonard Cohen**

Samson sat by the pool in bright sunlight at his Caribbean island estate, in a bathing suit and sunglasses at a table with an umbrella over it, reading a newspaper. A servant served him a drink. Isaac and Buddha walked up and pulled up chairs.

"Sam," Isaac said. "We gotta talk."

"We're bored," Buddha said. "Life's too easy here."

Samson put his newspaper down on the table "You too, Isaac?" he asked. "You getting tired of lying on the beach every day and having sex with beautiful girls every night?"

"Man, it's like being on vacation," Isaac said. "After a while you want to get back to work."

"Yeah," Samson agreed. "I always wanted to be disgustingly rich, but it came too quickly. I can't stand this."

A few days later, Samson, the president, Delilah and three secret service agents rode in an open limousine in a ticker-tape campaign parade in New York City. Samson and the president waved to the cheering throngs. The president was in good spirits, as the strategy of embracing Samson and abolishing the IRS breathed new life into his re-election campaign, and helped him surge in the polls.

As they rode slowly down the street, the pregnant woman whom Samson had helped, no longer pregnant, carrying the baby in her arms, dressed in white, bathed in light and looking supernaturally radiant, approached the limo and threw Samson a flower. Samson stood up, turned to her and reached out to her. He hadn't forgotten her prophetic words, all of which had come true, and he had wondered what became of her. She held out her hand to him.

"Who *are* you?" he shouted.

She tried to answer, but the car moved on and the crowd surged forward, leaving her behind. Samson remained standing, looking for her, but she was lost to view. Although Samson didn't see him, Elliot Mess was also in the crowd. Samson sat back down next to the president, with Delilah seated on his other side. He took his wallet out of his pocket, removed a check, and turned toward the president.

"Mr. President," Samson said. "As agreed, I have a cashier's check for seventeen point eight billion dollars payable to the U.S. Treasury Department. I wanna give the money back."

Delilah grabbed his arm from behind him, her nails digging in, trying to stop him from handing over the check. "I knew it!" she said. "I knew the president wasn't lying. You're the one who was lying. You lied to me!"

"I didn't lie," Samson said. "I didn't tell the truth, but I didn't lie."

"Who said I was lying?" the president asked.

Delilah pointed at Samson with her thumb. "He did!"

"Actually, Mr. President," Samson retorted. "I didn't say you were lying. All I said was that you're a politician, and I said that politicians lie. Both those statements are factually correct. Delilah put those two statements together and incorrectly inferred that I was saying you were lying."

"You're splitting hairs," Delilah asserted. "You intentionally misled me."

"You don't understand the situation," Samson said, yanking his arm free from her grasp, the check still in his hand.

"Don't do it, Sam! Don't give it back! What's wrong with you? Why ruin everything?"

Samson had sworn confidence to John Keister and had not explained to Delilah why he had no choice but to give the money back. "I didn't earn it. I don't want it," he said. This feeble explanation only served to further enrage Delilah.

"You didn't earn it? You don't want it?" she mocked. "Want kind of schmuck *are* you? *I* earned it. *I* want it. I figure I have some say in this. If it weren't for me you'd be in jail and you couldn't have gotten that money."

"If it weren't for *you*, I wouldn't have needed it."

"*I* got you into the IRS computers."

"Yeah, you also got me arrested."

"*I* got you the plane."

"Yeah, well next time try getting me one with rear-mounted guns."

"I lost my job, I risked going to jail." She started sobbing, something Samson had never seen her do before. "I lost my husband. Okay, never mind that part. I risked my life to get that money. And now you're going to give it back for no reason? And you didn't bother to tell me?"

"Yeah, just like you didn't bother to tell me you were married to Elliott Mess."

"Ooh!" she said. She started girl punching him with her fists about the chest and shoulders. He let her do it for a moment, but when it started to hurt, he grabbed her arms. She stopped hitting him, and backed away. "If you go through with this, you'll never see me again," she said.

Samson knew it wasn't just the money for her. It was the money. But even more than the money, he knew she was painfully disappointed that Samson wasn't the man she thought he was. She saw his giving the money back as a wimp out. What she didn't understand about him was that he wanted to win the Monopoly game by winning the Monopoly game, not by stealing money from the government. And he wanted to get back in the game, in the United States, not spend the rest of his life sunbathing in the Caribbean.

"If all you care about is the money....," he said, "then, frankly, my dear, I don't give a damn."

"You took that line from Gary Cooper," the president said.

"You're kidding, right?" Samson asked.

"It wasn't Gary Cooper?"

"Clark Gable."

Samson reached out to hand the president the cashier's check. Delilah grabbed his arm, yanked it backwards, and tried to get the check, causing a strain in his shoulder. Samson tried to pull free and she tried to bite his arm. He pushed her away hard and she almost fell. Samson went ahead and gave the president the check. Delilah, in disgust, stood up, jumped out of the slow-moving limo, and ran off into the crowd. Samson's jaw dropped. He stood up and looked for her, but she quickly got lost in the crowd.

"Boy, you really pissed her off," the president observed. "She's a babe. You shouldn't let her get away."

"Maybe I should have kept the money."

"Yeah, you should have."

"You're right. Give me the money back." Samson reached for the check, but the president pulled his arm back.

"I don't give money back," the president said.

"Look, I changed my mind," Samson said.

"You said you didn't give a damn."

"I was bluffing, okay?"

"I guess Shakespeare was right: 'Pussy *doth* make cowards of us all,'" the president said.

"That's not what he said."

"What *did* he say?"

"'*Conscience* doth make cowards of us all?'"

"That's not true, certainly not in politics. 'Pussy doth make cowards of us all.' That makes a lot more sense."

"Yeah, whatever. You're right. But I don't care about that. I just want the money back."

"I already told you, you're not getting the money back." The president shook his head "no."

Samson looked from side to side, then suddenly lunged toward the president. He put one hand, open handed, up against the president's face and pushed his head back. At the same time with the other hand he grabbed the cashier's check out of the president's hands. Secret Service agents sprung into action.

The driver raised the convertible top on the limo and started speeding off. The other agents grabbed hold of Samson. One of them got him in a headlock, and pulled him off his seat, while two more worked on his arms. Samson tried to hold onto the check, but he was forced to drop it as one of the agents twisted his arm behind his back. They held him, as the president bent down, picked up the check, and smiling at Samson, put it in his shirt pocket.

Chapter 34

Samson and Delilah

*"Oh here, come over here… Between the traitor and her pain
Once again, once again, Love calls you by your name."*
—**Leonard Cohen**

"A rich man is nothing but a poor man with money."
—**W. C. Fields**

In the months that passed after Samson gave the money back to the president, there wasn't a day when he didn't think about calling Delilah. But he resisted the temptation. Samson understood Delilah. It would be easy to dismiss her as a superficial broad who only cared about the money. But Samson knew it went deeper than that. It wasn't the money; it was the guy who got the money. He knew she had a primordial attraction to him because he was tough, virile, and self-confident, and what they had in common was that they both viewed money as the way you keep score in the monopoly game of life. She liked Samson because she saw him as a guy who knew how to win that game. And when she saw him wimp out and give the money back to the government, it didn't compute. It seemed inconsistent with the character of the guy who wasn't afraid of IRS agents, prosecuting attorneys, and judges; who wasn't afraid to escape from a prison sentence, steal a plane, steal billions from the IRS, and go to war against the entire U.S. government. She didn't get it. Samson instinctively understood this. And he also understood there was no way he could persuade her he'd made the right move. He figured she wouldn't find anybody better than him, and when she realized that, she'd miss him and come back.

The Spoilsport Motors car lot was soon back in business and looked the same as ever, filled with the usual assortment of clunkers and pimpmobiles. Buddha no longer worked there. His parole had ended, so he was free to work on the Internet again. He had started an online consulting business, advising companies how to defeat hackers. Based on the formidable reputation he gained after successfully hacking the IRS system, and with referrals from his influential new friend Karl Rogue, business was booming.

One day Delilah, looking as hot as ever in a fancy summer hat and sunglasses, drove into the Spoilsport lot in her Thunderbird, the convertible top down. Isaac ran over, excited to see her. She stayed sitting in the car, the engine running.

"Delilah," Isaac said. "I never thought I'd see you here again. Did you wanna sell that old T-bird?"

"I wanna see Sam," she said.

"I thought you said you never...."

"I know what I said," she interrupted. "Where is he?"

"He's not here anymore. I own this place now."

Delilah, stressed out and in a hurry, put the car in reverse. "Where is he? I've gotta warn him!"

"Warn him? About what?"

Delilah got Samson's new address from Isaac, and guided by her GPS she raced over, and soon found herself parking in front of a large, and rather fancy Rolls/Maserati dealership (like the one the author of this book will be shopping at after this book makes the *New York Times* bestseller list). The dealership had rows of Rolls Royces, Maseratis, Ferraris, and other fancy cars outside and inside in the showroom. Delilah got out of the car, and looked around in awe, trying to figure out what Samson was doing at this place. She walked into the showroom and wandered past salesmen showing cars to customers. She asked one salesman who wasn't busy and he pointed her down a hallway to Sam's office. She heard Sam's voice from out in the hall, and peaked in the door. He was seated at his desk, talking to a customer who stood in front of him, and he didn't see her.

"Mr. Samson," the customer said. "You understand that I can't purchase that Silver Cloud right now."

"Uh-huh," Samson said.

"I'd like to get a refund of my five-thousand-dollar deposit."

"We don't give refunds."

"Look, the state just put a tax lien on my business. So I can't afford the car. I want my money back."

"We don't give money back. The contract says all deposits are nonrefundable."

"I know what it says. But I feel very strongly about this."

The customer moved forward aggressively and suddenly reached into his pocket. Samson leapt to his feet and put his hands in the air, expecting a gun. But the customer was only reaching for some documents, apparently as proof of the tax lien. He leaned forward and showed the documents to Samson. Samson put his hands down, took a wad of cash from his pocket, counted out $5,000 in hundred dollar bills and handed it to the customer. The customer shook Samson's hand, then turned around, and recounted the money. As the customer put the money in his jacket pocket, and turned to leave, Samson snuck up behind him, and started to reach into his pocket to snatch the money back, but he was distracted by a familiar voice.

"Hey," Delilah said, "how'd you like to take me for a test drive?"

The customer walked out, the money still safely in his pocket.

Samson looked up, startled, and turned to see Delilah. She walked in and came very close to him, her breasts brushing up against him, just like the first time she saw him. He noticed that she was even wearing the same perfume. "What are you doing here?" he asked. "I thought you only like billionaires."

"I missed you, ya big schmuck. What are you doing working here?"

"Working here? Do you think a place like this would hire me?"

"You don't work here? What, you *own* this place, Sam? Where'd you get the money?"

"For a smart broad, Delilah, you're awful dumb."

She backed away just a little. "I don't get it."

"Do you know how much the return on investment on seventeen point eight billion dollars, invested in a diversified portfolio of mutual funds and corporate bonds, with an average annual yield of eight percent over a four-month period is?"

Delilah saw a calculator on his desk. "Okay, let's see," she said. "That was what, did you say eight percent annualized on seventeen point eight billion dollars over four months?" She did the calculation. When the result, $475 million, printed out, her eyes lit up. She put her arms around his neck and held her body close to his. "I love you, Sam."

Samson and Delilah walked out of the building together. A Rolls stretch limo pulled up in front of them. One of Samson's employees rushed over to open the door for them. They got in the back seat. The driver was Pete.

They drove off, holding hands, into the sunset, happily unaware that Elliott Mess was following in the car behind them.

"I am for a government vigorously frugal and simple… To preserve the people's independence, we must not let our rulers load us with perpetual debt…. For this is the tendency of all human governments… til the bulk of society is reduced to be mere automatons of misery... Then begins, indeed, the war of all against all…. And the fore horse of this frightful team is public debt. Taxation follows that, and in its train wretchedness and oppression."

—Thomas Jefferson

"The right of the people to be secure in their persons, houses, papers, and effects, against unreasonable searches and seizures, shall not be violated..."

—4th Amendment, United States Constitution.

Afterword

Although this story is fictional, it contains some factual tidbits. The story about Congressman George Hansen, who Samson tried to locate and then found out was in jail, is entirely factual. Hansen was, in real life, a seven-term congressman, who held hearings on IRS abuses of power and wrote a book about it, *To Harass Our People*. Hansen was then sent to federal prison, purportedly for a minor violation of House Ethics rules, failing to report assets owned by his wife on his disclosure form. You may have noticed that Congressman Hansen wrote a blurb for **The Taxman Cometh**. (See page ii)

Congresswoman Geraldine Ferraro, the 1984 Democratic candidate for vice president, engaged in the same ethics violation and was not prosecuted. If a dubious criminal prosecution of a congressman, who dares to go against the IRS, makes you wonder about the status of free speech in America, it will be interesting to see if the government also finds some pretext to come after the author of this book.

The Bank Secrecy Act of 1970, cited by Elliott Mess, is a real law that allows the Treasury Department unfettered access to all your bank and credit card records, and requires all banks to notify the Treasury Department of large cash deposits (over $3,000) or large cash withdrawals (over $5,000), or any other "unusual" currency transactions. The IRS really does have ultra-constitutional powers to seize money, assets, and property without prior court hearings or anything remotely resembling due process of law.

As mentioned by Samson at his trial, former Senate Majority Leader Tom Daschle, former House Ways and Means Chairman Charles Wrangle, and former Treasury Secretary Timothy Geithner, are all real government officials and known tax cheaters, who faced no federal investigation or prosecution.

Everyone has seen the tags on mattresses warning that it's a violation of federal law to remove them. The Energy Policy Act of 1992 is a real federal law that outlaws selling showerheads that have a water flow greater than 2.5 gallons per minute, and toilets which use more than 1.6 gallons of water per flush. The Energy Independence and Security Act of 2007 is also a real federal law that prohibits the sale of incandescent light bulbs. All of the examples of frivolous, excessive, and wasteful federal spending given by Samson during the trial are real and factual, including the millions spent by the IRS itself on useless conferences and silly videos.

Although there are, as far as I know, no unmanned drone aircraft in operation over the United States as of the time of this writing, the FAA has issued regulations permitting future domestic operation of drones. By the time this book is published there could be thousands of drones legally spying on American citizens, on behalf of local police departments, federal law enforcement, and other government agencies. NPR really did broadcast a report, just like the one Samson heard on the radio in Chapter 3, that the Department of Homeland Security has plans to purchase 600 drones for domestic use. No explanation was included in the report as to what the drones would be used for. Spy satellites are already in operation over the United States and can be used to locate anyone who has a cell phone or GPS device. Video surveillance cameras operated by private businesses and government agencies are omnipresent in schools and in our cities, and are rapidly proliferating.

The IRS commissioner's reference to a million square foot government data mining facility in Utah where hard drives are collecting data on everyone in America is, astonishingly, also factual. Even George Orwell could never have dreamed of such a monstrosity

In his opening speech in Chapter 1, the IRS commissioner makes the statement: "The simple principle 'from each according to his ability; to each according to his needs' is the foundation of modern civilization." If this quote has a familiar ring, it's because it comes from Karl Marx. It is a description of the central economic principle of communism. Today the statement could just as easily be a popular slogan for the Democratic Party, as it defines the essential philosophical foundation of redistributive justice and the welfare state in modern America.

Having explained the factual information woven into the story, I want to clarify that the bit about Darth Vader, I mean Darth Nader, being the IRS commissioner is fictional.

I hope my readers will forgive me for lacing with philosophical arguments what otherwise might have been a more entertaining story. You may be able to figure out where to find me on the great ideological divide, or perhaps more accurately, the great ideological continuum. However, I did try to present some semblance of the other side of the argument, not, I concede, to be fair – I don't care about being fair - but so as not to appear too manipulative. I have less interest in indoctrinating readers than in provoking thought. I could have portrayed persecuting attorney Phil S. Stein and IRS Commissioner Darth Nader as blithering idiots. Instead I allowed them to make moderately articulate arguments for statism, even though I think people who believe in statism actually *are* blithering idiots.

Perhaps it's overkill, or flogging a dead horse, or some other overused metaphor, to be explicit, but in case you missed the point, let me spell it out. For those readers of a liberal, or progressive, or whatever other term is used these days, persuasion, you deserve credit for your charitable impulses. Your philosophy of social democracy, a redistributive notion of social justice that underlies the social safety net and the welfare state, is based on compassion, a redeeming human trait. The problem with social democracy is that there's a price to pay for all this compassion.

On its face, social democracy is a plausible ideology, but even liberals/progressives have to recognize the tradeoff when public policy is based on compassion. When politicians use the term "compassion" they mean taking money from people who have it, and transferring it to people who don't. This "compassion" is directed at those who receive largesse; there is no compassion for those from whom the money is extracted. The enormous transfer of wealth necessary to sustain the welfare state inevitably requires a massive tax burden on wage earners at every level; taxes on the super-rich won't even begin to cover the costs.

The welfare state requires a humongous, and horrendously inefficient, bureaucracy not just to collect the taxes, but to hand out the goodies at the other end of the process to those whom politicians have targeted for beneficence. But people don't, as a general rule, pay taxes because they want to. All tax collection systems have to be based on the threat of force. Creation of the modern megastate requires that we the people cede an enormous amount of power to politicians and unelected government officials. If the IRS didn't have ultra-constitutional powers to seize your house, your bank account, and your car, and to throw you in jail, you wouldn't pay. Okay, maybe *you* would pay because you're an unusually altruistic and high-minded person with a hypertrophied sense of civic duty, in other words, a sucker. But you're the only one. No one else would pay.

The paradox of liberalism is that liberals think of themselves as anti-authoritarian free spirits, who like to live in a free and open society where wildness is valued and anything goes. This may have been true in the romantic early days of liberalism, when liberals were out of power and anti-establishment. But today liberalism *is* the establishment. And the policies liberals support are all about regulation, domination, bureaucracy, and authority, and about extending government control over every aspect of human behavior except sex. Liberalism isn't liberal anymore; it has transmogrified into totalitarianism.

My question for liberals is this: Do you believe that the politicians and bureaucrats who are empowered by a political economic system based on redistributing wealth are more compassionate, honest, and altruistic than the rest of us? Or do you believe that government officials are just as opportunistic, self-interested, and greedy as us ordinary folk? If you feel these officials are just as selfish as the rest of us, how can you think it's safe to entrust them with the extraordinary power to decide from whom to take money, and to whom to give it? Where can you find angelic people to administer this much power without the graft and corruption we invariably see when men have such power over other men?

The reason that billions upon billions of dollars of special interest money floods into Washington to corrupt our political system is precisely because government now has this unbounded power over us and our money. If government didn't hand out trillions of dollars in goodies, do you think anyone would bother to hire lobbyists and buy off politicians with campaign contributions? If you want to know the price we pay for social democracy, go answer your front door; Elliott Mess is there about to ring your bell.

On the other hand, if I've persuaded any liberals that you'd rather live in a free society where we don't have guys like Elliott Mess ringing our doorbells, and guys like Darth Nader laying their meglomaniacal plans for ever-expanding bureaucracy under their own control, perhaps you might consider rechanneling your altruistic feelings of compassion for the needy into *voluntary* charities, where those laudable charitable impulses will do less damage than they do under the authoritarian and corrupted system of *mandatory* charity known as the welfare state.

Abraham Lincoln once introduced Harriet Beecher Stowe, the author of anti-slavery classic *Uncle Tom's Cabin*, as the woman who started the Civil War. If *The Taxman Cometh* frees millions from oppression by doing to the income tax what *Uncle Tom's Cabin* did to slavery, my reason for being will have been fulfilled.

Jim Greenfield

THE END

Critical Book Review

For the sake of dialogue, critique from a different perspective:

"Only in the perfervid imagination of a tea-party anarchist like Jim Greenfield could the hero of a novel be the 'twenty-seventh richest man in the world,' a lemon-selling used-car salesman who deals solely in cash, specializes in fraud, doesn't do refunds, and considers it his patriotic duty not to pay taxes for seventeen years. In this addled, sexist, politically incorrect book—as subtle as Ayn Rand, as nuanced as a sledgehammer, and as likely as *Sharknado*—the only interesting segments are the parts dubbed "Optional" when Greenfield actually expounds on the flawed philosophy behind his Randian views.

Although Greenfield is ridiculously paranoid about the Internal Revenue Service (and IRS Commissioner Darth Nader), some of his wild conspiracy theories do hit a bit too close to home. Warrantless government spying on American citizens in the era of the NSA, elected officials who do only what special-interest lobbyists legally pay them to do, and digital ballot-counting without a paper trail are just a few of the Orwellian realities that liberals and conservatives should join together to thwart. Without the ridiculous plot and gratuitous sex and violence, this could have been an interestir polemic and not a cartoon. But *THE TAXMAN COMETH* prefers snark over legitimate debate. It thus well represents the current intellectual state of the tea-party movement."

– Mark Levine, liberal talk radio host and former Legislative Counsel to Congressman Barney Frank (D-MA)

Jim Greenfield's Reply to Mark Levine's Humor-Challenged Critique:

"As likely as *Sharknado?*" "Wild conspiracy theories?" "Prefers snark over legitimate debate?" Hey, Mark, it's not a debate. It's a *novel!* It's *fiction!* It's *satire!* It's not supposed to be "likely." Get it? You probably thought *Star Wars*, and *The Matrix*, and *Young Frankenstein* were "unlikely, wild conspiracy theories" too. Or for that matter, how about *Hitchhiker's Guide to the Galaxy?* How *likely* was that? Or *Hamlet*, an unlikely story about a guy sent on a mission to murder his uncle by a ghost claiming a "wild conspiracy" of assassination against the king?

Mark Levine claims he graduated magna cum laude from Harvard, and went to Yale Law School, so I guess he's smart, but he clearly lacks the perspicacity to recognize great literature. To put his sardonic commentary about this masterpiece, *The Taxman Cometh*, in context, bear in mind that Mark made similarly dismissive remarks about the complete works of Shakespeare. Okay, not really; that's satire also. Maybe they don't teach satire at Harvard.

Mark accuses me of being "ridiculously paranoid" about the IRS, as if that were possible. Apparently he's oblivious to what the IRS does to real people in the real world. See, Mark, these people make a living seizing other people's money and property; putting people in jail, and scaring the shit out of the entire population. Is it paranoid to point out that people who are out to get you are out to get you? We'll see if Mark feels the same way after his first IRS audit, which won't happen to such a prominent liberal as long as his fellow Democrats are running the country.

And speaking of preferring "snark over legitimate debate," what does calling me a "tea-party anarchist" sound like? Does that fall under "snark," or is it "legitimate debate?" Apparently neither Harvard nor Yale taught Mark the meaning of "anarchist" either. People like Mark Levine, who think they are "liberals" but are actually totalitarians, are prone to conflate constitutionalism with anarchism. By the way, Mark, I'm not involved in the tea party movement. But I do believe in the same principles of limited constitutional government and individual liberty that the founders of our nation believed in. So if I'm an anarchist, what about Washington, Jefferson, Franklin, Hamilton, and Madison? Were they anarchists also, Mark? Try reading "The Federalist Papers." Anarchists don't found nations. Anarchists don't write constitutions. Anarchists don't create governments and write laws. It's a glaring self-contradiction to accuse constitutionalists of anarchism, a frequently used, and desperate ploy by the extreme left, intended to obscure the fact that they no longer believe in the United States Constitution.

For more dialogue go to blog at www.taxmancometh.net.

About the Author

Jim Greenfield graduated from Cheltenham High School in suburban Philadelphia, where he played football with future Yankee slugger Reggie Jackson. Jim was a government major at Cornell, where he made the Dean's List, and was a columnist for the Cornell Daily Sun. He received his J.D. from Penn Law School in 1974, practiced law in Philadelphia, and then in Oregon. Jim opened several used car dealerships and a finance company. You'll notice that the hero of *The Taxman Cometh* is a tax cheating used car dealer. This is mere coincidence as Jim swears the story is not autobiographical.

In the 1980s Jim began investing in real estate. In the 1990s Jim launched a controversial career as a talk radio host, having programs on several Portland area stations, including

KVAN, KUIK, KKGT, KBNP, and KOHI, and on two syndicated networks, the Liberty Network and Talkstar. Jim was fired as a talk host seven times, which he claims was because he was too good. He brags he was fired more times than any other host except Rush Limbaugh, the difference being that Limbaugh now makes $32 million a year. See www.jimgreenfieldshow.com.

Jim served for eleven years on the Board of the Goldsmith Greenfield Foundation, and six years on the Selection Committee for the Goldsmith Prize for Investigative Journalism at the Kennedy School of Government, Harvard University, where he worked closely with directors Marvin Kalb and Alex Jones. Jim ran for Congress in Oregon's first district in 2002 and 2011. He was soundly defeated, which Jim attributes to his unfortunate habit of telling people what he thinks. Jim has done better as a businessman than as a politician, and has a substantial portfolio of investment properties. Like the hero of *The Taxman Cometh*, Jim doesn't like the government because he doesn't like a bunch of bureaucrats, who aren't as smart as he is, telling him what to do.

The Taxman Cometh – the Movie

Coming soon to a theater near you….
if you're smart enough to put up the money!

If you think this novel should be made into a movie, and you'd like information about a Hollywood film production of *The Taxman Cometh*, as an investment, please visit www.taxmancometh.net, and click on the link for movie investment info. (This is not a solicitation for investment nor an offer to sell securities.)

How About We Abolish the IRS?

If we get rid of the income tax, we can finally say, in the words of Martin Luther King, "free at last, free at last, Thank God Almighty, I'm free at last!" If you're interested, please go to www.taxmancometh.net, and click on the link for "21st Century Abolitionists," a citizens' movement to abolish the income tax forever.

The Taxman Cometh **Blog is at: www.taxmancometh.net**